Chasing Her Dream

Jennifer Slattery

🌿
LOVE INSPIRED
INSPIRATIONAL ROMANCE

LOVE INSPIRED®
INSPIRATIONAL ROMANCE

ISBN-13: 978-1-335-75877-4

Chasing Her Dream

This edition published by arrangement with Harlequin Books S.A.

For questions and comments about the quality of this book, please contact us at CustomerService@Harlequin.com.

Love Inspired
22 Adelaide St. West, 40th Floor
Toronto, Ontario M5H 4E3, Canada
www.Harlequin.com

Recycling programs for this product may not exist in your area.

Printed in U.S.A.

We love him, because he first loved us.
—*1 John* 4:19

To Amelia, guard your candle, sweet girl;
God's got amazing plans for you.

Acknowledgments

Behind every book is a large number of people who helped make it happen. Jodie Bailey, thank you so much for your keen insight as you read each phase of this book and offered suggestions on how to make it stronger. I also want to thank Lynn True Blood and SmartPak Equine's Ian Macartney for answering my plethora of horse-related questions. I also want to thank Lynn Hummer from the Pregnant Mare Rescue for sharing her knowledge and experiences with me. Joe Rickley from Farm Bureau, thank you for answering all my flood-related questions! And as always, thanks to my awesome husband, Steve, and sweet daughter, Ashley, for your continued support. Love you much!

Chapter One

Rheanna sat staring at the Literary Sweet Spot while her car engine quietly ticked. "What if we made a mistake, Ivy?"

Her friend clutched her binder to her chest. "Adding paleo options? I know we might not get many sales among Sage Creek's meat-eating ranchers. But I have no doubt coffee shops and naturopathic stores in Austin will be all over these things."

"I'm not talking about your health food business."

"*Our* business. We're in this together."

Only because Ivy had nagged and cajoled Rheanna into saying yes to the venture. And because Rheanna had lacked the courage to move her and her daughter to Sage Creek, to run a ranch of all things, by herself. Besides, Ivy had stood beside her during some really tough times. When Rheanna learned of her husband's affair, Ivy had been a rock through that heartbreak and the subsequent divorce.

Still, Rheanna's primary goal was to save the ranch. Everything else came second. "I'm talking about the horses. What do we know about managing stock and boarders?" Clearly not near enough, considering their stalls were over half-empty, their foal sales were pathetic and they couldn't seem to keep reliable staff.

"That, my friend, is why we're here." Ivy grabbed the job posting flyers from the back seat and handed them to Rheanna. "I'm certain there's at least one strong, capable cowboy needing work in this town. Besides, that's why we need to pour our energy into our protein bars. Once our health food business takes off, it'll more than compensate for all our financial concerns." Loaded down with samples and promotional material, she got out with a grin.

Rheanna stepped out from her vehicle and into the mid-summer, Texas humidity. In this heat, thinking about all the chores waiting for them back at the ranch made Ivy's suggestion to focus more on the health food project and less on the horse business appealing.

They hurried into the busy, air-conditioned café and waited for Leslie, the new owner, to finish with a string of customers. Then, while Leslie and Ivy met back in her office, Rheanna found an empty table near a magazine rack to sip her chai latte.

She had a sinking feeling her and Ivy's plans were way too complicated. Two women running two different businesses from the same location and using, in many ways, the same funds, often robbing one business to pay the other business's expenses.

"Hey, little lady." Mr. Farmer, an older man who lived ten miles outside town, came up beside her. "Saw your flyers. You're looking for more help?"

She sighed. "New help."

"What kind?"

"We need a riding instructor." Preferably one who also knew how to train foals or could supervise those who did.

"What happened with Geoffrey?"

She suppressed a snort. "He got in another bar fight and the other guy pressed charges."

"Sure wish he'd get his act together soon." He pulled a toothpick from his shirt pocket and placed it in his mouth. "If I hear of anyone horse-handy in need of a job, I'll send them your way."

If she had a dollar for every time someone had said that to her, she'd have enough for that stable roof repair she needed. Were all the cowboys happily employed, or had the ranch's reputation scared everyone off? Unfortunately, she suspected the latter, a reality not helped by the fact that her great-uncle, whom she'd inherited it from, had been such a crude crab apple.

She would cut her losses and sell the place, if she and Ivy hadn't banked everything on making this work. And Rheanna had uprooted her six-year-old daughter, an act that caused a good deal of tears. She couldn't disrupt her world again.

The door behind her chimed, and she turned to see a much-too-familiar-looking cowboy walk in. Her pulse hiked a notch when his light brown eyes met hers.

Bearing a striking resemblance to Chris Evans, Dave Brewster stood maybe six foot three inch, and his frame, which had always been on the muscular side, had filled out considerably. A dusting of sable-colored whiskers covered his square jaw. Based on the way his eyebrows shot up when his gaze met hers, he was shocked to see her, as well.

She stood, immediately transported to her sixteenth year and her cancer diagnosis. She hadn't heard of Hodgkin's Lymphoma before. Her mind had struggled to make sense of it all—the long battle that lay ahead, the lifetime of follow-up appointments, the ongoing risk of secondary cancers. In a moment, her entire world had shifted. Oh, how she'd longed for someone to stand beside her, someone to lean on. She'd felt so very alone.

Dave had abandoned her, with little more than a good-bye, when she'd needed him most.

"Rheanna. It's been a spell, huh?" He wore faded jeans, a snug T-shirt and a cowboy hat.

"Yeah." She swallowed, fighting back feelings of rejection that surged as fresh as the day he'd left. "How have you been?"

He studied her for a moment, as if debating how to answer. He gave a slight shrug. "I'm hanging in there."

"I... Are you... I thought you moved? Are you back?"

Another pause. "I'm here for the Mooney wedding."

He and Will had stayed in touch? Her stomach soured to think he'd maintained contact with someone he'd barely considered a friend, but not her, whom he'd once claimed to care deeply for. Yet more confirmation that she'd truly meant nothing to him.

"Where are you living now?" Why was she engaging him in conversation? To prove she no longer cared? That she was unaffected by his presence? That his leaving hadn't completely devastated her?

"Cheyenne, Wyoming."

"The Cowboy State." Sheriff Unice, who seemed to have an ear in every conversation, gave a low whistle from where he stood by the display counter. "I hear y'all are pretty waterlogged." He picked up a newspaper and tucked it under his arm. "Least, that area was a few months ago. All that flood mess receded yet?"

"In some places." Sorrow clouded Dave's eyes.

"Those poor ranchers." Unice shook his head. "Don't know how they'll bounce back after such a loss. I doubt many of them have insurance to cover it." He meandered off to read his paper, leaving Dave and Rheanna to their painful and awkward reunion. At least it was for her. Dave, on the other hand, appeared as confident and unaffected as ever.

"You here visiting your uncle?" His voice held a bite on the last word, resurrecting questions she'd long since forgotten, the biggest of which was—why had he and his family really left, all those years ago?

One day, they were living on the ranch, renting land from Rheanna's uncle; the next, they were gone.

"My uncle died just under a year ago. Alzheimer's." Technically, from aspiration pneumonia, a complication caused by his disease. She tried to avoid questions related to him, whenever possible. Too many awkward conversations followed. A lot of people had made it quite clear how they felt about the man, and by association, the ranch.

"I'm sorry to hear that."

She couldn't gauge the sincerity of his words, nor should she care. He might've been the first to leave, but he wasn't the only one that had moved on.

"Hey, Rheanna?" The sheriff strode back toward her, his expression tense. "What's the biggest trailer you got?"

"Five horse."

"Think you can bring it out to Larry Hart's property? We've got an emergency rescue situation and need all hands, and vehicles, on deck."

"I'm not familiar with that location."

"I know where it is," Dave said.

The sheriff gave one quick nod. "Mind going with her? Showing her the way?"

Rheanna's stomach tumbled, and her gaze shot to Dave. Talking with him here, briefly, and in a public place, she could handle. Sitting in a vehicle with him, driving down some quiet country road, would trigger too many memories. Old emotions she had no intention of allowing.

Dave's golden eyes remained fixed on her. "Sure."

"Perfect." The sheriff clamped a hand on Dave's shoulder. "I'll round up a few more guys and will see you out there in a few."

A jittery sensation swept through her midsection, suggesting her heart was in danger. Only she wasn't a naive high school girl anymore, nor could she be fooled by Dave Brewster's disarming, boyish grin. He'd hurt her once. Deeply. She would not allow him to do so again.

Dave swallowed, gaze locked on Rheanna's deep, espresso-colored eyes. He'd known, coming back, there was a chance he'd see her. Figured she might return for the Mooney wedding, as well. But standing here now caused the ache of losing her to burn afresh.

Soon, she'd be riding in his truck, like old times, only with way too much history between them.

At nearly a foot shorter than his six-foot-three self and weighing maybe a buck twenty, she'd filled out in all the right places. She wore her hair long. Her curls framed her oval face in loose waves, the dark brown matching her eyes. The woman was as beautiful as ever, if not more so.

Did she ever think of him? Wonder what might have been, had her uncle not betrayed Dave's dad? Did she even care about how he and his family had been treated? Or had her lying uncle convinced her they deserved it?

Such questions wouldn't do him, or the horses they needed to rescue, any good. He scratched his jaw. "You ready?"

"I came with my roommate." She scraped her teeth across her bottom lip and scanned first the café then the book area extending beyond it. "I'll be right back."

She darted off to talk with an older woman, who sat in

a paisley armchair near the magazines. They spoke briefly, then the woman glanced his way and nodded.

Rheanna returned. "Okay. We can go."

He beat her to the truck, hurried to clear junk off the passenger seat and opened her door for her, like he always used to. Back in the day, she'd responded to his chivalry with a shy vulnerability tinged with trust that he'd found endearing.

Now she hesitated and visibly tensed beneath her formal smile. "Thank you."

Her response stung, though he knew it shouldn't matter. They both needed to leave the past right there, in the past, and focus on the task ahead. Then they could return to their respective lives, him to his fight to save the ranch and her to whatever occupied her time.

With a deep breath, he rounded the vehicle and slid behind the wheel.

Her perfume, fruitier than he remembered, filled the cab and temporarily stalled his senses. She'd always had that effect on him, from the first day he'd met her.

It'd taken him years to get over her, longer before he even considered dating again.

She buckled her seat belt. "You remember how to get to my place?"

"Your place?" He eased onto Main Street and followed a yellow two-door out of town.

"I inherited my uncle's ranch."

His eyebrows shot up.

She laughed. "Don't look so surprised."

"Just figure that's a lot to handle is all."

She opened her mouth like she wanted to say something but then shrugged and gazed out her side window.

Was she thinking about any of the letters he'd sent, of

his declarations of love and promises of their future? Had she even kept them?

He suspected not. Like her uncle had said the day Dave came to the house to tell her goodbye—girls like Rheanna didn't end up with guys like Dave. The fact that he'd spent the better part of a decade turning his life around wouldn't change that. Especially since he was back in Sage Creek much like he'd arrived the first time, broke. All his hard work, saving every dime to build a ranch, steed by steed, wiped out by Wyoming's spring floods. Worse, he couldn't do anything until the waters receded.

Rebuilding would be akin to starting over, only harder, considering all the cleanup that lay ahead.

What if he couldn't? If the expense and devastation were too much?

That simply wasn't an option. Not after all his dad had invested, sacrificed, to help Dave buy the ranch in the first place. He wouldn't let his father down, no matter how many storms, literal or figurative, came at him.

As they neared the Green ranch, the place he'd sworn he'd never set foot on again, he tensed. The sign hanging from the arch over the entrance was weatherworn and lopsided, its protective stain long gone, as were the flowers that once surrounded the posts. He turned onto the former gravel road, now a long stretch of dirt dotted by deep potholes.

The once lush pastureland on either side now stood dry and overgrazed, with maybe a quarter of the horses he would've expected to see. The fences were in dire need of repair. The house paint was peeling and many of the roof shingles were buckling. Clearly, the old man's business had taken a turn for the worse. Considering how he'd treated Dave's family, served him right.

Only this place belonged to Rheanna now. Regardless of how much she'd hurt him, she deserved better than this.

"Can you stop here a minute?" She rotated toward the house, hand on her door. "I need to check on my daughter. Make sure my friend Lucy is okay watching her a bit longer."

Daughter? His gaze shot to her bare ring finger. Was the kid's father still in the picture?

He shifted to Park. "Sure."

She got out, hurried up the porch steps and disappeared into the house.

What was her daughter like? Did she resemble her mama? How old was she? How did she and Rheanna act around each other?

Rheanna's mother hadn't been the best role model. He couldn't count all the times and ways that woman had hurt her and pushed her aside for her latest in a long string of boyfriends. All the times Rheanna had cried on his shoulder and the protective urge that had stirred within him.

He'd promised he'd never hurt her like that, only he had.

An image from what felt like a lifetime ago came to mind, unbidden. It was of her, riding across the pasture on Bella, her palomino. She'd looked so happy, as if nothing existed except her and the mare.

The horse she'd loved and lost, because of him.

The door to the house opened, and Rheanna reappeared wearing mud boots and a cowgirl hat, hair back into a ponytail. Her flushed cheeks, likely from hustling about in the midday heat, only added to her beauty.

She climbed into the truck and shut her door behind her. "Sorry about that."

"No biggie." He wanted to ask her about her daughter, to understand just how much Rheanna had changed and who she was now. But in knowing, he'd risk falling in love all over again.

"The trailer's back by the east stables." She pointed.

He nodded and continued past a fork in the road leading to the ranch hand cabins similar to the one he and his folks used to live in, past the indoor arena, another stretch of pasture and an old tractor partially overgrown with weeds.

Unfortunately, the trailer had a flat tire. By the time he got it changed and the rig hooked to his truck, he wondered if maybe the rescue operation would be over.

"How long you been back?" Rheanna adjusted her visor to block the low-riding sun.

He turned onto the main road leading toward San Marcos. "Just got in today."

"Quite the homecoming, huh? Getting wrangled into a rescue operation."

"Not sure I'd call this a homecoming." Dave veered onto the shoulder to let a fast approaching car pass. "Last I remember, you were trying to talk your mom into letting you get into show jumping. Anything come of that?"

She gave a soft chuckle. "Not really."

"How come?" He'd promised to help teach her and had even started creating something of a course, using wood and other materials he found lying around. He'd been looking forward to the excuse to spend more time with her. Her uncle had given his family the boot less than a week later.

"I guess I sort of lost interest."

That didn't sound like her. He'd always admired her quiet determination and strength. Though she'd been as sweet as apple butter, when push came to shove, her shove pushed back. With how often she'd talked about wanting to compete in horse shows, he couldn't imagine her simply getting bored with the idea. Then again, he thought

her interest in him would last, was something real, too.
She'd sure seemed to move on quick enough.

"What have you been up to?"

"Ranching, riding, training."

"For a living?"

He nodded.

"Wow. That's impressive."

The fact that her admiration meant so much, even now,
frustrated him. If he wasn't careful, his heart would dive
back into emotions he'd worked long and hard to kill.

"How's your mom handling the winters? From what I
remember, she wasn't a fan of the cold. She used to wear
gloves to church whenever air-conditioning season hit."

"My folks stayed in Texas. Bought a grocery store
about thirty minutes northeast. What about your mom?
Did she ever—" *Marry that guy she was always shoving
you off for.* Not a question he should be asking, not unless
he wanted to prick old wounds. "Where'd she end up?"

"This month?" She gave a wry laugh. "Florida. As to
what she's doing, I wouldn't know."

In other words, her mom wasn't any more interested
in talking with her than she had been all those years before. His time in foster care had well introduced him to
the sting of parental rejection. Praise God, he'd found the
sense of family his young heart had always been searching for in his folks. He'd experienced such healing once
the adoption went through.

He slowed, watching for the dirt road leading to the
Hart property. He wasn't surprised to find the entrance
even more overgrown than he'd remembered. Rumor said
Larry had a drinking problem—and quite the mean streak.
Apparently, both had caught up with him.

Pebbles pinged the truck's undercarriage as Dave continued on to a dingy white-and-gray, double-wide mobile

home with peeling trim. Beyond that stretched a neglected pasture dotted with tall mounds of what looked like blackberry bushes. A band of trees stood along the far edge of the property.

A handful of trucks and trailers lined the sagging and broken barbed wire fence to his right. The sheriff, standing in front of a group of men, appeared to be giving instructions.

He glanced in Dave's direction, said something to the guys, then walked over while the others dispersed.

Dave stepped from his vehicle with a tip of his hat. "Sheriff."

The man gave a nod, first to him then to Rheanna, who now stood beside them. "Thanks for coming. We've got quite a job on our hands. Fifteen, maybe twenty horses. Probably more hiding in the trees, some in worse shape than others."

Dave rested a hand on his belt buckle. "Who called this in?"

"A gal over yonder." The sheriff motioned toward a border of trees to their west. "From the sounds of it, the horse owner beat his wife pretty bad. She got free of him some kind of way, ran to her neighbors and called the police. When they came out to investigate, they found a bunch of abused and neglected horses."

"The males gelded?"

"Some. Not all."

Dave had worked with enough stallions to know this operation could turn dangerous real quick. "That'll be interesting." He cast a glance at Rheanna, hoping she'd have the sense to stay out of harm's way.

"You say that like a man who knows from firsthand experience."

He shrugged. "These horses we're going to get now— where are we going to take them?"

"Not sure. One of the fellas is making calls." His phone dinged. He checked the screen, then returned his cell to his back pocket. "I bet the guys could use some extra muscle getting the geldings loaded into trailers." He studied Rheanna. "Think you could coax the younger ones out from the woods? Figure the babies might respond best to a female voice."

Most likely that'd be true for all the animals, considering they'd been abused by a man.

Rheanna nodded and headed toward a thicket of trees some of the men had disappeared into. Dave could only hope—and pray—that the guys would keep an eye out for her safety. If he'd thought all this through, he would've talked her out of coming in the first place.

But his brain hadn't been working right. It'd been too stuck on their past.

A past he'd do best to forget about.

"Hey, son."

He turned to find two men, one tall, the other short and thickly built, fighting to get an emaciated pregnant mare into a trailer. "Think you can help us out?" The taller of the two motioned him over.

A visual of Mona, one of his broodmares who got swept away in the flood, flashed through his mind. She'd been such a sweet girl. Easy to train, loyal and pregnant with her first foal. He should've known the levy would break. Should've moved all his horses well out of harm's way.

Dave shook the image aside and ambled over. The horse's ears swiveled back and forth, her front legs splayed, muzzle tense. Poor girl looked terrified, and rightly so. Who knew what kind of treatment she'd experienced at the hands of a human?

The tall guy stood inside the trailer and was trying to pull her forward while his friend stood behind her flapping his arms in an effort to get her in.

Dave inched into the mare's line of sight. "Hey there, Mama." He kept his voice low and calm. "You're all right. Everything's all right."

The man's phone dinged, and he checked the screen and answered. "Yeah?" He mumbled something. "Hold up." He looked at the mare, then made eye contact with Dave. "Think you can manage her for a bit? One of the stallions is acting crazy."

"Yep." The horse looked too skinny and weak to cause much of a problem. Based on all the ruckus behind him, the other fellas couldn't say the same.

"You take her lead." The guy hopped out of the trailer and handed the rope to Dave. "We'll go help with that angry steed thrashing about in the stables." He motioned for his buddy to follow him, leaving Dave alone with the mare still outside the trailer.

"Guess it's just you and me, little lady." He leaned against the trailer. "I'll probably have to force you in, with the help of those fellas that just strolled away." Although he was hoping that wouldn't be the case. "But for now, let's just hang."

What was Rheanna doing? Knowing her, she was soothing a frightened filly or mama, and likely doing a much better job at that than he was.

The men didn't return for nearly thirty minutes, and by then, the mare almost seemed comfortable. At least, until the taller guy started flapping his arms again.

The sheriff ambled over. "Hoping to hear on a location soon." His phone rang, and he glanced at the screen. "Might be our answer now." He answered and listened to whoever was on the other line.

Dave scanned the horizon for a glimpse of Rheanna. She stood talking to a stocky man in a straw hat a few trailers down. Her body language suggested she wasn't happy, nor should she be, seeing the results of such obvious neglect.

"Sounds like a plan." The sheriff ended his call and turned to Dave. "Problem solved. Those gals out at Emmitt Green's old place got room."

Dave took in a breath.

Rheanna's ranch, the property Dave had once considered home. Where he'd first fallen in love and where his heart had later shattered in two. In some ways it made sense she'd offer her place. From what he'd seen, she had plenty of room. But did she have the capacity to care for abused animals? Hopefully she'd already considered and had a plan for this.

He had the capacity, the wherewithall to help. He'd rehabbed animals before. But could he do so without falling back in love with the one woman he would've done anything for?

Until her loud silence proved he wasn't what she wanted.

Chapter Two

Rheanna tensed as she watched the string of trailers ahead of her and Dave turn at the entrance to her ranch. "Um, where are they going?"

Dave cast her a sideways glance. "What do you mean?"

"All those men and horses. Why are they stopping here?" Did they need more trailers or something? That didn't make sense, not unless they thought more horses remained hidden in the trees. If that were the case, surely they would've said something.

"Didn't you talk with the sheriff?"

They veered onto the gravel road dissecting her two east pastures. "About?"

"Unice said y'all had offered your place. That you had plenty of empty stalls to house these creatures."

"He what?" She stared up ahead to where the trailers, at least five of them, were gathering. Obviously, this was the result of miscommunication. "I'll call him." Only she didn't know Unice's number. She doubted Dave did, either.

"Seems just as easy to talk to him in person." Parking, he motioned toward the group of men gathered in front of her barn, Ivy standing front and center.

"Excuse me." She jumped out of the truck and was immediately accosted by a brisk wind that whipped her hair about her face and dust into her eyes.

Gravel and twigs crunched under her boots as she marched toward the group.

She reached Ivy and the pack of men out of breath, in part from her quick stride but mostly from apprehension. She'd been friends with her roommate long enough to know that she tended to act before thinking things through, driven by emotion more frequently than logic.

"Hey." Rheanna placed her hands on her hips and scanned the people gathered on her property. T-Bone, her dog, bounded up to the men one at a time.

"Sit." Rheanna pointed a finger to the ground, and the dog obeyed.

She caught the tail end of a conversation between two men to her right—something about the vet coming out to gauge the horses' body scores and help them plan nutrition.

A group of the men started unloading skittish and severely malnourished horses from the trailers while Ivy directed them into the stables.

"They're clean and ready to go." She picked up an empty bucket and tossed it out of the way.

The nausea Rheanna had felt back at the other ranch returned as the men led animals that looked near death past. Ribs, hip bones and spines sticking out, sharp and angular. Dull eyes, and heads that appeared too large for their emaciated bodies.

"Stop." Rheanna raised a hand, palm out.

The men stopped midstride and turned to stare at her. She planted a hand on her hip. "Ivy, what's going on?"

Ivy gave a slight shrug. "The horses needed somewhere to go, and, well, we've got room."

"No offense, ma'am." An older gentleman with long

gray hair that curled up from under his dusty hat widened his stance. "But nursing starved horses back to health takes more know-how than you'll find on the internet. Feed 'em too much too quickly, and you could kill them."

His friend nodded. "Seems counterintuitive, I know. But the extra calories can spike their insulin, which throws off their electrolytes. Not to mention the vet needs to figure out if there are any other reasons these here horses are so thin." He motioned toward the trailers behind him. "Pretty sure Doc did an initial assessment of most, if not all, the horses back at the Hart place."

Rheanna rubbed her temple. "We're not equipped for that." They had enough challenges trying to manage their ranch with healthy horses as it was.

The man with the gray hair scratched his jaw. "You saying you won't let them stay?"

Her mind struggled to catch up. "We're understaffed and tight on funds as it is." These horses needed someone skilled in dealing with abused animals. Even then, half of these horses might never allow a human on them again. It'd be near impossible finding people to adopt horses that weren't rideable. "What will they eat? Who will pay their vet bills?" Their medical care alone could wipe her out financially.

"The community will pitch in." The sheriff gave a quick, firm nod, as if his statement settled the matter. "Sage Creek folk have always been good about that."

"And if they don't?" The horses wouldn't be much better with her and Ivy than they had been prior to the rescue. "Then, not only would they go unfed, but we'd be short—" shorter "—on resources to care for our herd. Where's the vet?"

"I suspect he'll be here soon." The man with the gray hair crossed his arms and rested them on his protruding belly. "He's dealing with a situation having to do with an aggressive stallion back at the other property." He paused, and his gaze intensified. "But like I done asked a moment ago, you telling me they gots to go? Because if that's what you're fixing to say, just spit it out so's we can figure out what to do next."

Rheanna released a breath. "Like I said, we're short-handed already."

Dave glanced around, then back at her with his jaw set. "I can help. For now anyway."

Dave Brewster, a man who clearly held sway over her heart even now, if her quickened pulse was any indication, working on her ranch? Interacting with her, every day? "I…"

"You got a place to quarantine them?" The potbellied man wiped his sweaty face with a handkerchief.

Rheanna gave a hesitant nod. Her stables on the far side of the property were completely empty. That was how bad business had been, and taking on a bunch of rescues wouldn't help turn things around.

But neither could she, in good conscience, send them away.

Ivy smiled. "Sounds like we've got a plan."

Rheanna shot her roommate a glare. "It's not that easy."

"Yeah, it is." The gray-haired guy crossed his arms. "You got space, and these starving, near-death horses got no place to go. You need grain and special feed, extra vet care for them? Whatever it is, we'll work it out, won't we, fellas?"

Affirmatives resounded.

Rheanna frowned. "And if you don't? Then what?"

Silence followed.

"Mama?"

She startled and turned to see her daughter's big brown eyes staring up at her.

"Why don't you want them?"

"What, sweetie?" She dropped down to eye level and took her daughter's hand.

"That man. He said no one wants them, not the mamas or the babies. Is that true?"

"It's hard to place this many horses, sweetie. They need a lot of space."

"But there's room here. You don't want them, either?"

Tears pricked her eyes as a conversation from six months prior came to mind. Amelia had overheard Rheanna venting about her daughter's biological father—about how he'd never wanted to have a child in the first place. That he'd started pulling away from her, and likely making plans to leave, the moment she became pregnant.

Amelia had blamed herself for her father's leaving. Having never met her own father, Rheanna understood her daughter's pain. Although Rheanna did her best to explain her ex-husband had simply been selfish and irresponsible, she knew her daughter felt abandoned.

Rheanna took a deep breath and gave Amelia's hand a squeeze. "Sweetie, it's just..." More complicated than her six-year-old heart could comprehend. She stood and turned to Dave. "You'll stay to help with the horses?"

"Yeah."

Butterflies did acrobats in her stomach. She could not, would not, fall back in love with that man. No matter how many loopedy-loops her heart did whenever he turned those big golden eyes her way.

"We'll need to quarantine the rescues." She rubbed the back of her neck, gazing toward her partially filled stables. "I'll have to shift some things around, get all my boarders moved to the east stalls so that those on the west side are free."

"No problem."

The way he said that, the words themselves, instantly brought her back to all those summer days he popped in to help her with Bella. Seemed that horse was always getting into a bind or fighting a trick. But whenever Rheanna grew frustrated, unexpectedly Dave appeared and shot her that relaxed grin that always made her pulse stutter. Whenever she asked for his help, his response had always been the same. No problem. Back then, she'd believed him. Believed he'd stick around, and with him around, that everything would be all right.

Until he left, taking his false promises with him.

Having him here, entrusting such an important role to him, was a bad idea. He hadn't exactly shown himself to be reliable, nor had her heart proven trustworthy around him. But what choice did she have? Those horses needed help. "How long do you think you'll be able to stick around?"

His gaze intensified, sending a flutter through her midsection. "Long enough."

In other words, potentially too long for her good. She couldn't—wouldn't—endure another heartbreak.

While Dave helped the men get the horses settled, his mind kept drifting to Rheanna. This was a mighty big ranch for her to run on her own, although she always had been a hard worker. Never one to complain or ask for favors. He still remembered the first time he saw her, the cute girl from the city. Dressed in white shorts and a lavender top, with her curls blowing in the wind, she intrigued him in a way no other girl had.

Although Dave's dad rented land from her uncle, he'd

never had cause to cross property lines. Not until he met Rheanna. Then he found every reason to head her way, volunteering to check and fix their fence line being his favorite excuse.

Coaxing a frightened foal toward a back empty stall, Dave froze, hit by a surge of guilt as memories rose up.

The men had put the pregnant mare in Bella's old stall. Most every morning when he'd ventured this way, all those years ago, he found Rheanna standing right in that space, grooming her horse. Often, she'd be singing, so soft you'd never hear her unless you were up close. Then she'd catch Dave watching her, and her cheeks would blossom with the most beautiful blush.

Reminding him of how precious, how sweet, she was. Much too sweet for a troublemaker like him. While, thanks to Jesus, he'd changed, ranchless and penniless as he was, he still wasn't the man she deserved. He'd do well to remember that.

Metal clanked against wood, and the foal jerked his head and ears back.

Dave tightened his grip. "We're okay, little fella." He spoke in a calm, even voice and kept his body relaxed. "No one's going to hurt you here."

He understood the animal's fear. He'd felt the same way when his social worker dropped him off at his would-be parents' house. She promised he'd be safe, that they were kind and would take care of him. He hadn't believed her. It took a long time for him to learn to trust.

He expected the horses to walk a similar journey.

Could he stay that long? As much as he wanted to, he had his own ranch to save. But if he left too soon and these animals died…?

He wouldn't be able to live with that.

His throat felt scratchy, and he cleared it.

With a bit more prodding, he finally got the pretty little gray in a stall and closed the gate. Peeking in at the others on his way back to the trailers, he called his buddy back in Cheyenne.

The phone rang numerous times before Mitch picked up. "Hey. How's the Lone Star State treating you?"

Dave relayed all that had happened.

"Wow, dude. That's a lot. How long you plan on staying?"

He scratched his chin. "Depends on when she can get qualified help out here." It wasn't like he was in a hurry to get back to Cheyenne, with his land still underwater. Except that he needed to figure out what to do with it— and his remaining horses, which were currently on his buddy's property. "I'm thinking…you interested in adding to your herd?"

"You wanting to sell?"

"Might have to." He needed to know all his options.

"How many were you thinking?"

"Whatever I need to in order to pay for food, vet care and boarding."

"All right. Let me crunch some numbers and get back to you."

"And if you wanted to help me breed my stallions—" he had two "—I'll let you keep half the stud fees. You can breed my mares, too, and keep half of whatever the foals sell for."

"I can't ask for that."

"It's only fair, considering all the work and risk involved. Plus, you'd be doing me a big favor."

Rheanna approached, holding her daughter's hand, and the image of them together, of Rheanna's tender, maternal side, stirred strong emotions within him.

He ended his call with his friend and, tipping his hat at Rheanna, slipped his phone in his back pocket.

"Hi." She tucked a lock of hair behind her ear. Her dog ambled up from behind and parked himself at her feet. When she paid him no mind, he rubbed his head against her leg, and she smiled and patted his head.

"Hey." He rested his hand on his belt buckle, his gaze shifting from the beautiful woman before him to the brown-eyed child gazing up at him. The little one wore her hair, also brown though streaked with blond highlights, divided into two braids. Her bangs hit just above her brows.

"This is Amelia." Rheanna gave her daughter a sideways squeeze, and pure joy lit the girl's face. "She's six, about to enter first grade."

Her contagious smile triggered his. "Hey there, princess."

"Hi!" Her grin widened, and she straightened, as if he'd just called out her inner royalty.

"You lending a hand with all these horses?"

She nodded. But then she cocked her head, brow furrowed. "Who are you?"

"Dave's an old friend." A hint of sorrow shadowed Rheanna's expression, and her gaze dipped for a moment. "He's here to help."

"Your family, too?"

He shook his head. "Just me."

"You don't have a wife?"

"Nope."

"How come?"

His gaze shot to Rheanna, and his face heated. He'd almost married once. He got engaged a few years ago to a lady who decided she wasn't cut out for ranching life. She realized how much she wanted to live in the city, and he knew he'd never fit there. The fact that they could end things so easily proved to them both that their love wasn't strong enough to last. He was glad they figured that out before they said their vows.

Rheanna cleared her throat, looking as uncomfortable as he felt. "Sweetie, that's not our business."

Amelia looked between them. "Oh. Is that a secret?"

"What?" Rheanna's cheeks flushed pink. "Of course not. It's just…" She released a sigh. "Never mind."

Amelia turned back to Dave, standing a tad taller. "Aunt Lucy says I'll bring the hurt horses joy, same as I bring her and Mama."

"I bet you will."

She twirled the end of her braid around her finger. "Do you want to hear a joke?"

Dave grinned. "Sure."

"Why do horses wear shoes?"

"Um… Because they lost their ballet slippers?"

She giggled. "No, silly. Because they need to run superfast, like me."

He laughed. "Of course."

"Do you know why the mouse became friends with the dog?"

He and Rheanna exchanged an amused smile. "Hmm… He wanted to share his biscuits?"

She shook her head, her braids swishing across her shoulders. "The cat was being too mean."

"Makes sense."

"Where did the robin go for vacation?"

"Mr. Dave and I need to get back to work." Rheanna placed a hand on Amelia's back. "Can you save your jokes for dinner?"

"Okay." She studied Dave. "Are you eating with us?"

He stammered, common sense warring with an almost gut-reaction desire to say yes.

Rheanna's blush returned, and her gaze faltered. Did that mean she wanted him to join them, or preferred he didn't?

He shifted his weight. "I imagine these horses will keep me busy enough." He wasn't trying to be rude, but neither did he want to put Rheanna on the spot or make things more awkward than they already were.

The girl's brow furrowed. "That one with slobber, is she going to die?"

"What?" His glance pinged to Rheanna.

She brushed her bangs aside with the back of her hand. "I was planning on talking with you about that. One of the rescues has something going on with her mouth or jaw. I know they're all pretty thin, which likely means they weren't fed. But she might have something else going on that's keeping her from eating. Hopefully she just needs her teeth floated. The vet said he'd come and take a look as soon as he could."

Floating horses' teeth was a simple process of filing down rough edges with a rasp called a float. Like Dave, she hoped that was the mare's only problem with eating.

"He coming out pro bono?"

"I hope so. But I didn't ask. I know those guys said everyone would help me out, but I'd like to know how. I mean, it's not like this is a recognized charity. I'm pretty sure, legally, we can't accept tax-deductible donations."

He wondered the same thing. These horses were going to need care for some time before they'd be ready for adoption, assuming that day ever came.

Amelia plopped onto the ground and started drawing in the dirt with her finger.

Rheanna gave her head a pat, then walked past her. "Well, let me show you around. Where we store the grain, the hay, keep important numbers and all."

"I have been here before." Although intended as a joke, he regretted his words the moment they came out.

"I'm sure things have changed."

More than she might've realized. Then again, something in her eyes suggested she knew, or perhaps worried, how this place might appear to him, having last seen this place at its peak. She had to feel overwhelmed, now more than ever.

"This is the office, same as when you were here." She motioned toward an opened door to her right and the small, cluttered room beyond.

"I remember." He eyed the binders covering the small card table that functioned as a desk, same as when old man Emmitt owned the place. "Guess you and your uncle ended up growing pretty close, huh?" He wasn't sure how he felt about that. Sure, the guy might've been different around her, but he was still a slimy snake. Hadn't she been able to see that? Then again, with how uninvolved her mother had been, Emmitt had been about Rheanna's only family.

"Not really." She picked up a Coke can, shook it, then tossed it into the garbage. "I don't have a clue why he left this place to me. I can't really say I came to know him all that well. He wasn't really the relationship type, you know?"

"True. Though you did spend numerous summers out here."

She shrugged.

As in three total? He remembered the first time she'd come and twice more after that. Did that mean she hadn't visited since that July Dave and his family had left?

"As you can see." She made a sweeping motion with her arm and stepped back into the aisle. "I didn't exactly inherit a thriving business. You can probably understand why I'm concerned with taking on these rescues."

He nodded. "I'm sure people will help, drop off food and whatnot." Otherwise, she and the horses would be in a heap of trouble.

"For how long? What happens when these horses don't feel so urgent anymore and everyone forgets about them or sort of trickles away?"

"How hard would it be, to file for nonprofit status?"

"Meaning, to remain a rescue facility long-term?"

He hadn't thought about it like that, but considering all these horses, and all their needs, she'd need to do something. "Want me to check into it? See what your options are? A buddy of mine leads a ministry outside town a ways. He might know."

She sighed. "That sounds complicated."

"We'll figure it out."

"We?" Her tone sharpened, and her eyes narrowed.

"I'm here to help, Rheanna. I won't leave you hanging."

She didn't respond right away. "I suppose I have no choice but to believe you."

She never used to talk to him like that, look at him like that.

What had her uncle said to turn her heart against him? Enough to cut him off completely, back when she'd been his world, and now to treat him like...like...

Like the walk-away kind.

His gaze shot to the sweet little girl, still drawing in the dirt.

Where was her daddy?

Maybe Rheanna's edge wasn't about him. Maybe whatever had happened between her and Amelia's father had left her jaded.

If so, the horses weren't the only ones spooked and in need of healing.

Chapter Three

Rheanna used to love weddings. The flowers, lace and promises of forever love. But after her failed marriage, every ceremony she attended felt like salt on still-raw wounds.

"Mama!"

Rheanna startled and jabbed her eye with her mascara wand as she sat leaning into the mirror above her vanity. Tears, likely to be soon streaked black, flowed down her cheeks. And just when she most wanted to appear presentable.

She needed the locals to begin to see her as a competent businesswoman. Granted, social events weren't exactly the place to make boarding propositions, but she could at least form some networking connections. Though no one treated her as such, she couldn't help thinking everyone viewed her as an outsider, in the local horse community especially.

She grabbed a moist towelette and turned to face her daughter, who'd barreled into the bedroom, chanting her name. "What is it, dear?"

"Do my hair, please?" She held her hands under her soft

brown locks on either side of her face, looking so adorable Rheanna couldn't help but laugh.

She didn't have much time to spare, especially considering she now had to completely remake her face.

The last time Dave had seen her, she'd been a mess after a long day of mucking stalls. But tonight, she wanted to look beautiful. Make him regret having walked away all those years ago. Or at least, she hoped to lessen her sting of rejection, which felt fresh whenever he was around.

"Mama!" Amelia gave a dramatic slump and crossed her arms. "Please! I want to be pretty, like you and Aunt Ivy."

Rheanna smiled and pulled her daughter closer. "You are, sweet girl. And Mama's running late."

"I've got you, girlfriend." Ivy leaned on the door frame, garbed in a rather loud outfit. She wore a polka-dot dress with a thick purple belt and yellow wide-brimmed hat.

"Yay!" Amelia squealed and jumped up and down, nearly knocking herself off-balance. "In upside-down French braid buns?"

Rheanna brought Ivy Amelia's soft bristle brush with a smile. "Thanks."

Ivy looked her up and down, eyebrows raised. "Girl, you might want to tone that down some."

Rheanna frowned. "What's wrong with how I look?" Her off-the-shoulder, scoop-backed teal dress hugged her waist, but not outlandishly so, and the bottom hem hit below her knees.

"Nothing, if you don't mind snagging the attention of every man at the reception. That might not help you gain their wives' business. Which reminds me... I want to tuck some of our product brochures in my purse."

"Um, no."

"Why?"

"You're seriously not planning on spamming wedding guests, are you?"

"Of course not. Mentioning our delicious yet healthy and eco-responsible treats when the opportunity arises? Absolutely."

"Please don't." Rheanna grabbed her perfume, stood, spritzed the air and walked through the spray.

"Seems no different than what you're doing."

How could Rheanna explain the subtleties of networking to a woman who was anything but subtle.

She sighed. "Just remember this is a wedding, and neither you, I, nor our business goals are the center of attention."

"Oh, you go dressing like that, and you'll be the center of attention all right." Ivy winked.

Rheanna's mind jumped to Dave, and her face heated. She rolled her eyes. "Whatever."

Why did she keep thinking of him? Obviously, he'd moved on the moment he and his parents had left Sage Creek.

Besides, she had much more important things to worry about—like bringing in income, a goal now complicated by the fact that nearly half her stalls were filled with rescue animals.

Rheanna finished getting ready, then hurried into the kitchen to heat up frozen fries and chicken strips. As usual, T-Bone followed and hovered near the oven.

"Eat your own dinner, silly." Rheanna pushed the dog away to keep him from burning his sniffing nose.

"Come here, boy." Amelia patted her thighs. She sat at the table while Ivy stood behind her, fighting to braid her hair from the bottom of her scalp up.

"You sure feed this kid a lot of junk." Ivy spoke over a rubber band in her mouth.

Rheanna suppressed a huff. She was all for healthy living, but unlike her roommate, she wouldn't be enslaved to the idea. "She can have carrots with her meal."

Ivy mumbled something about creating habits, but a knock from the living room cut her off.

"Aunt Lucy!" Amelia sprang from the chair, jerking her hair out of Ivy's hands, and darted off.

Rheanna followed and opened the door with a smile. "Thank you so much for coming."

"Spend the evening with this sunshine?" Lucy Carr, an older woman from church, winked at Amelia. "Sure, hurt me some more."

Ten minutes later, those two were deeply engrossed in a dominoes activity, and Rheanna was ushering Ivy out the door. "We're going to be late."

"You worry too much." She inspected her nails as she walked to the car.

"No, I like to prepare." Rheanna slid behind the wheel and ignited the engine. The low fuel light came on. "But apparently not well enough."

"Oh." Ivy peered over her shoulder. "Sorry about that." Her car needed repairs she couldn't afford, so she'd borrowed Rheanna's that morning to drive to Austin and back.

She sighed. "It's fine. I'll fill it and you can pay me back."

A while later, they walked into Trinity Faith Church as the organ started to play the wedding march. Rheanna scanned the audience for Dave, then chided herself. How would she ever manage having him around the ranch every day if his being in Sage Creek had already dominated her thinking?

He's not interested in you. He's no good for you. He never cared for you.

Maybe if she kept telling herself that, her heart would get the message.

"Here." Ivy pulled her toward a back-row pew that allowed direct visibility to Dave across the aisle and about halfway up. "Ah. The groom wrote his own vows."

Rheanna thought back to the morning she and her ex stood at a similar altar, pledging to hold tight to one another "until death do us part." Promises. Easy to make, and break. Both he and Dave had demonstrated that.

After the ceremony, Rheanna grabbed her purse and inched toward the aisle behind an older couple. The flow of people soon bottlenecked so that she found herself eye to eye with Dave.

"Hey." He wore dark jeans and a black vest over a white button-down shirt, which was likely as dressed up as that cowboy got. His gaze swept the length of her, his expression showing a hint of admiration, or perhaps curiosity.

"Hi." Why did she feel so jittery all of a sudden?

"How's the little mama?"

She frowned. "What?"

"The pregnant mare?"

Oh. Of course. "She's eating some, so that's good. But she's real skittish. Won't hardly let anyone near her."

"That could be a problem when it's time for her to foal."

She'd thought of that. "The vet was out this morning. He left some detailed instructions and things to keep an eye on."

Once outside, the people in front of them dispersed, some migrating toward the bridal party or their cars while others gathered on the church lawn.

One of Dave's old buddies from school caught his attention and pulled him into a discussion with a group of guys.

Where had Ivy disappeared to? Rheanna glanced about

and located her friend marching toward two twentysome-
things lingering near a car.

Recognizing the determined set of Ivy's jaw, Rheanna
hurried to cut her off en route. "Hey. You ready to jet?"

Ivy frowned and looked from Rheanna to the couple,
then back to Rheanna. "What's your hurry?" She shoved
brochures into the outside pocket of her purse.

"Just figured we could snag a seat." Her gaze drifted
back toward the church, landing on Dave. He was still
talking to the group of guys he used to hang out with on
occasion. More connections he'd managed to maintain?

She was being way too sensitive. Every conversation
he held didn't indicate his loyalty toward others and rejection of her.

Ivy laughed. "Girl, it's about time."

"What're you talking about?"

She smirked. "Oh, you know." She looked at Dave with
raised eyebrows.

"Hardly." If she ever did become romantically involved
with anyone again, and that was a big if, she'd make certain the guy was ready to commit, not just to her, but
Amelia, as well.

Dave parked in a marked field and followed the plunk-
ing of a banjo into a barn turned banquet hall. Dark wood
lined the floor, and rustic-looking tables draped with linen
and nearly all full, stood end to end along the wall.

Tea lights hanging from the rafters and support beams
lit the dim interior. He searched the shadowed space for
a vacant chair. He never knew how to act at events like
these, wasn't good at the chitchat most everyone engaged
in. At least he could occupy himself with eating.

His gaze landed on Rheanna, looking as beautiful as
ever in a soft blue-green dress. Auburn-streaked hair cas-

cading over her shoulders, she sat with her friend a few tables from the front. The other seats at their table were full.

"Here he is now."

He turned at the sheriff's deep voice and tipped his hat.
"Sir," he said, then nodded to the men with him.

Unice made introductions. "This here's Liam's kid. You
remember him, right? Used to rent land out at Emmitt
Green's place. Where we brought them horses yesterday."

"Bet that was a surprise, huh?" One of them, a guy with
bony shoulders and ears that poked out from beneath his
hat, shook his head. "That place sure ain't nothing like it
once was. Don't know what those little ladies were thinking, taking on the ranch, though I doubt they expected it
to be so run-down."

The man's buddy scoffed. "You know how those city
folk can be. They spend a week or two out here, mosey up
to some horses and think they've got ranch life figured out.
I honestly don't know how they'll keep that place open."
He cast Dave a side glance. "No offense, son."

Did these people associate him with the ranch now?
"None taken."

Eventually, the discussion turned to horse care, with
each man giving Dave enough "schooling" to fill a log-
book. They acted like they didn't think he knew what
he was doing, not that he'd let that bother him. He'd had
people doubt his competency before. That only fueled his
determination to succeed.

Rheanna got up, spoke to a waitress briefly, then
headed toward the bathrooms. He should say hi to her.
Seemed the polite thing to do, especially considering she
was technically his boss now. As weird as that felt. Besides, he could use an iced Coke.

He excused himself with a round of handshakes and

meandered toward the refreshments. There he lingered, glass in hand.

"Hey, cowboy." Ivy joined him at the drink table. "You got a thing for my friend?"

"What?" Heat surged up his neck. "No." Had Rheanna said something? "Why do you ask?"

"Oh, I don't know. Maybe because you've been watching her all night and practically followed her into the ladies' room."

He raised his glass. "I was thirsty."

"Right." With a slight smile, she took her drink, then sauntered off toward a group of women he vaguely remembered from high school.

Dave spent the rest of the evening trying not to look at Rheanna and averting his thoughts whenever they drifted in her direction. Instead, he thought about his flooded ranch, his pathetic financial situation and the pregnant mare back at the stables.

Experience told him mares preferred to give birth in privacy, and often at night. The abuse this poor mama had suffered would only exacerbate those tendencies, which could cause real problems in the event of a crisis. The chances of her labor going wrong seemed pretty high, potentially placing both mama's and baby's lives at risk. He needed to find a way to earn her trust before then. And to keep an eye out for signs of distress. Hopefully, she wouldn't deliver prematurely.

"I'll be. Dave Brewster, in the flesh."

He tensed at the syrupy sweet voice and swiveled to face the one woman he would've been happy to never see again: Sally Jo Nelson, Sage Creek's biggest flirt. "Ma'am."

They'd dated briefly in high school. She'd taken their relationship much more seriously than he had. He ended things when he and Rheanna started getting to know one another. Though Sally had managed to track him down and send him half a dozen or so letters and emails after he and his family had moved. Once the mail had stopped coming, he assumed that was the end of her.

"I heard talk you were back in town." She leaned toward him, head tilted. "Where're you staying?"

"Nice getup they have here." He glanced around. Might be a good time to get a drink. Except he was holding one. "How's the diner?"

"Good. You should stop by for some free fried chicken. Like old times." She paused, cocked her head and started to sway. "I love this song."

He took a side step, increasing the distance between them, and glanced about. Catching a glimpse of a rancher he'd been meaning to connect with, he tempered a grin. "If you'll excuse me, I need to talk with Cal Waldrip."

He darted across the barn, meandering around the now-crowded dance floor, before Sally Jo could protest or try to corner him into a meetup later. He spent the next thirty minutes peppering Cal, the most knowledgeable man on horse care in Sage Creek, other than the vet, with questions.

"What'd Doc Wallow say?" Cal popped a cream cheese stuffed olive into his mouth. "He expect them to pull through?"

"Some. But a couple of steeds are down at least 30 percent body weight."

The rancher released a breath. "Gonna be touch and go for a while. Probably the next ten days or more."

"That's why I wanted to keep your number on hand." He was gathering a list of folks he could call in an emergency. "The vet's been awesome. Did the initial assessments free of charge. But you know how busy he gets."

"Oh, I do. Why you think I learned all I did? Figure I about earned myself enough knowledge and experience for a degree. Stick around these parts long enough, you'll be able to say the same."

Dave had a feeling Cal was right.

"Want me to chat with her?" Cal tipped his head toward Rheanna, now sitting at a table covered with partially finished drinks and desserts. For the first time this evening, she was alone.

"I'll get her up to speed." That'd give him an excuse to talk to her. The fact that he was looking for that warned him to take a step back.

He'd loved, and lost, her once. He wasn't wanting a repeat. But they did need to build a working relationship.

"Thanks again." Dave shook the guy's hand, then, with a deep breath, approached the most beautiful woman in the room.

She glanced up, then straightened as he drew near. "Hi."

"Hey." He took the empty seat beside her. "Having fun?"

She shrugged. "You?"

"Like a root canal."

She laughed, and an awkward silence followed, pregnant with all the years that had stretched between them, everything they'd lost. They used to have plenty to talk about, at least she did. She'd chatter away about some book she was reading, some place she wanted to visit, her latest ride on Bella.

Rheanna had loved that horse more than anything. He frowned. He never should've had his friends over that night. They shouldn't have been drinking. The fact that he'd changed, had given his life to Jesus and no longer touched the stuff, didn't alleviate his guilt.

He should've told her. Maybe if her uncle hadn't given him and his family the boot, he would've.

"What about you?" She stirred her ice with her straw. "How'd you end up in Wyoming?"

"Work was easy to find, and I needed a job." Somewhere far from Texas, the state that held so many painful memories. "I got hired on by a local rancher, saved nearly every dollar he gave me."

It helped that the man had offered free room and board, in part because his land was so far out, there'd be nowhere for his help to stay otherwise. "Eventually, I bought my own place."

"You always did say you'd own your own ranch someday. Guess you made it, huh?"

"I'm not so sure about that." He told her about the floods. "It was like nothing I'd seen before. We had a wet spell, followed by a late freeze, then more storms. The soggy topsoil sat on solid ice. All that water had nowhere to go. Then the dam broke, releasing a surge of water that swept up chunks of ice. That's what hurt us most— all that ice, acting like a bunch of wrecking balls." His throat turned scratchy. "Took a bunch of my horses with it. Thank God the rest of my herd was on higher ground, but I couldn't get to them for days." He'd never felt more powerless.

Except for back in high school when his folks packed up their things to leave all they'd known, their livelihood.

"I'm sorry."

"It is what it is."

"Now what?"

His eyes stung. "Rebuild." Like he'd done countless times before. In the meantime, he'd been picking up jobs when he could, working as a ranch hand.

Movement in his peripheral vision caught his attention,

and he shifted to see Sally Jo heading toward him. His ears alerted to the band. The tempo had slowed, which meant...

He turned back to Rheanna. "Care to dance?"

Her eyes widened. "What?"

Way to act the fool. It was too late to take his words back now. Playing confident, he stood and held out his hand.

She looked from it to him before responding with a soft smile. "Sure."

Dave released the breath he'd been holding. "Yeah?"

She nodded.

Suppressing a grin, he led her onto the quickly crowding dance floor, telling himself this was no big deal. He was simply reconnecting with an old friend.

Who used to be so much more.

Based on the way his pulse accelerated when she placed her soft hand in his, time had done little to change his feelings toward her. *Why now, Lord?* He didn't have the mental space for romance. Besides, he wasn't going to stay long. As soon as Rheanna found someone to take care of the horses, he planned to head back to Wyoming.

Her sweet perfume threatened to stall his good sense. "Where's your princess?"

"At home watching movies with Lucy Carr. And likely eating enough popcorn to spoil her appetite for anything healthy for days."

"I remember Lucy. I only met her a couple times, but I heard plenty of folks talk about her. The way they tell it, the woman's Mother Teresa's twin."

"She's been great, offering to help with Amelia, making a point to connect with her on Sunday mornings, bringing casseroles to the ranch on occasion. When we first moved here, she and a couple other ladies from the church brought us a basket filled with food and lotions and such.

She said they were happy to have us in their community, though I'm not so sure everyone else agrees with them."

"What do you mean?"

"I get the sense folks aren't too happy we're here, is all."

Dave studied her. Was she experiencing fallout from things her conniving, no-good uncle did? That didn't seem right, although he could understand it.

"You return often?"

"To Sage Creek?"

She nodded.

"Nope. First time in years." When he left, he'd told himself he was never coming back. And yet, here he was. He gave her back a light squeeze, and for a moment, she leaned toward him, making him wish the song would never end.

But then she stiffened.

He glanced down at her, noting the way the overhead lights shimmered on her hair. "What's got you looking so serious?"

"Just thinking about the horses and how all this will affect Amelia. If she gets attached and…"

"We'll just have to make sure we don't lose a one, which is the plan."

"You've talked with the vet, right?"

"I know the prognosis isn't the best, but I've got to believe…" He swallowed. The back of his throat burned as memories from the night floodwaters swept away a chunk of his herd came rushing back.

Maybe helping to save the rescues would appease some of the guilt he carried from that catastrophic event.

She stopped in midstep. "Why did you agree to help me?"

He winced inwardly at the look of distrust in her eyes. "It was the right thing to do."

Though her expression indicated his answer left her with more questions, she didn't say more.

Someone bumped into his shoulder, alerting Dave to the fact that they were blocking the flow on the floor.

With a gentle tap to Rheanna's back, he guided her back into their waltz. "Remember Trista's thirteenth birthday party?"

"If I recall, that was the last place you wanted to be that night."

"True. My mom made me come." She'd been his foster mom back then. "I'd been living with her maybe two months, and she worried I was becoming a recluse. She said I needed to get out of my shell and start making friends. Guess she figured a cheerleader's birthday party would be the best way for me to do that."

"Well, Trista's folks had invited the entire high school."

"The very reason I didn't want to go." He laughed. "My memory says you weren't too thrilled with being there, either, the way you were sitting off by yourself."

"I guess I was lonely. That was my first summer at my uncle's, and I hadn't made any real friends. I mean, the girls talked to me during Sunday school and all, but the rest of the week I was pretty much alone."

"Until some ornery kid started hanging around."

"You weren't that bad."

"Only because I'd started watching myself. Trying to impress that pretty girl on the other side of the fence line, or more accurately, not scare her off." Short-term, his efforts had worked. But he'd lost her in the end.

Chapter Four

After church, Dave connected briefly with Rheanna to discuss her expectations and his role on the ranch. She'd encouraged him to move into one of the staff cabins, most of which, apparently, had remained vacant for some time. Living on the property would certainly help Dave's finances. Hotel fees added up quickly.

"I need to grab Amelia from her Sunday school class." Rheanna tucked her Bible into her bag and zipped it closed. "Want to meet me at the ranch?"

Dave nodded, then watched her join a group of parents headed down a blue hallway leading to the children's ministry classes. She seemed to be making a life for herself here.

His mom called as he was exiting the church. "Hey, thanks for getting back to me."

"Of course. Sorry it took me so long, but I lost my phone."

"Sounds normal." He chuckled. "Have you purchased your plane ticket yet?" Although he'd insisted she stay home and continue helping his dad in their little store, she'd been equally insistent she fly out to help him appeal

FEMA's denial of his claim. They'd deemed his application "ineligible," whatever that meant.

Every form and phone call felt like lemon juice on an open cut. There was no way to document a decade of hard work, of building a ranch from the ground up.

"I was actually going to take care of that this afternoon."

"Mind holding off on that a bit?" He climbed into his truck and snapped his seat belt.

"Why? Hasn't the water receded enough yet?"

"I suspect it will soon, at least enough that we can get in the house." He turned onto a residential street. "But I've got some things I need to tend to here in Sage Creek." He told her about the rescue operation, intentionally omitting where they'd taken the horses.

"When are you heading back?"

He paused. How would she feel, knowing he was staying on Emmitt Green's ranch? "Hard to say. Some of those animals are in pretty bad shape." And what about Rheanna's ranch? That place wouldn't last without a competent trainer. Integrity suggested he help her find and hire one.

"You always did have a big heart. I'm proud of you."

Proud of him. He wasn't sure why her words stung, except maybe because they felt so contrary to his situation. Ranchless, with more debt than prospects...

He would not let them down.

He'd been knocked down before and always found a way to climb out of whatever mess he'd landed in. He'd do so again.

He turned onto the two-lane highway leading to Rheanna's place. "I hate to keep you hanging, but can I get back to you later this week?"

"Of course. Take whatever time you need, son."

"Thanks, Mom."

He ended the call and drove out to Rheanna's, arriving at the staff cabins, set against a backdrop of trees, moments before her. She must've swung by the house to drop Amelia off first, because the child wasn't with her.

She parked to his left, got out and bounded up the steps. Holding his luggage, he met her on the stoop.

"Bill Goetz, our ranch manager, lives over there." Jiggling a key in the rusted lock, she motioned to the adjacent cabin. "He likes to keep to himself." She opened the door with a shove of her shoulder.

Dave stiffened as memories came rushing back. The space was near identical to the one he and his parents had once lived in. Bigger by maybe 500 feet, it had the same wood floors and paneling, same thick beams supporting the low-peaked ceiling, same stone fireplace occupying the far corner of the living room.

The loss he'd felt watching his mom pack up their things swept over him as he crossed to the glass sliding door leading to a treed backyard just like the one he'd sat in, as he'd struggled to make sense of it all—his new home, parents.

Trying to understand the people who had proved to him, again and again, that they valued relationship above all else.

Unlike Rheanna's uncle, and maybe Rheanna herself.

"I know it's not fancy, but it's clean, has running electricity, cable and Wi-Fi." She walked toward the counter dividing the living room from the kitchen and opened the cupboards. "You've got a coffeepot, microwave, dishes, silverware. Pretty much everything you'll need other than groceries."

She parted the blinds above the sink, then turned around. "I fix breakfast for all my staff by five thirty every morning, and you're welcome to join us for dinner every night. We usually eat around seven. I might not be able to pay much, but I can keep you well-fed. And if you take over the riding lessons, you can keep half of whatever you bring in."

"I assumed you wouldn't have much to spare, money-wise, after taking care of those rescues."

"I'm sure I won't, but neither do I intend to take advantage of you." She smoothed a lock of hair behind her ears.

Though not in the best financial position himself, he didn't feel right letting her assume all the risk. "Folks band together in situations like this." The fact that he had any horses alive now proved that. As he was currently on the receiving end of other people's kindness, it seemed he should show some of the same to Rheanna. "Wouldn't be right you shouldering all the burden here." Although he could help her build her student list easy enough. By month's end, his class schedule would be so full, he'd need to start a waiting list.

"Like I said, I can't afford much. But I'll pay what I can—at least, when it comes to working my horses. In regard to the rescues..." She paused and offered the shy hint of a smile that used to twist his insides, and maybe still did. "If you want to volunteer your time, I'd be more than grateful."

The vulnerability in her deep brown eyes drew him in a way he refused to evaluate. Hand on his belt buckle, he gave one quick nod.

She took in a visibly deep breath, and her obvious relief, which hinted at the load she was carrying, struck a compassionate chord within him. She had to feel overwhelmed—with the ranch, the rescues, raising her daughter, and all that while operating short-staffed. Yet, here she stood, readily taking it all on and revealing a strength he'd always admired.

Time had changed them both.

"How about if we go over all your duties?" She walked to the door, held it open and waited for him to join her.

"Sounds good."

"I'll drive."

Leaving his truck parked at his new, temporary home, he followed her into her silver, slightly rusted car. The interior retained her soft floral scent tinged with citrus. Sliding behind the wheel, she clicked on the engine, and children's Sunday school music filled the vehicle. She flicked it off and eased back out onto the dusty road.

Dave gave the property a visual sweep. He didn't see any ranch hands around. "How many folks do you have on staff?"

As they neared the pasture fence, her dog barreled toward her. After they got out of her car, the animal circled her before sitting and leaning against her legs.

"Bill oversees the care of the horses, pretty near the whole ranch, other than our riding academy. He's been here since long before I arrived. He works Monday through Friday, some evenings and weekends when needed." She scratched the dog behind the ears. "This here's T-Bone, our resident guard dog. If you're not careful, he may lick you to death."

He laughed. "Hey, boy."

"As to Bill, he's usually on call, but he had something he needed to do this weekend."

Bad timing.

She rested a hand on the fence railing and gazed toward her horses. There were eight, maybe nine, about half of them foals. "We've got one trainer intern—she's gone for two weeks, with her family. She's…" Rheanna scraped her teeth over her bottom lip. "She could use guidance. Our previous trainer taught her some bad habits."

"Such as?" Dave needed to know what kind of problems he might be facing with the horses, especially those used for lessons. What kind of untraining he might need to do, and how many of those poorly trained horses were used for lessons.

"Well, he pushed the horses too fast, for one thing. And the students, too."

"Chasing show points?" Though a history of wins could demonstrate skill, a person always had to prioritize horse and rider. But he'd seen a lot of trainers get caught up in the competition of it all, however, prioritizing horse shows over their clients. Granted, a string of ribbons displayed in the stables helped with credibility, but the instructor must always remain focused on their student.

Her expression tightened. "Among other things."

She didn't seem keen on sharing more, not that he blamed her. She was probably afraid, if she told him too much, he'd change his mind about hiring on. That made him wonder what kind of chaos he was stepping into.

But it didn't matter. Those rescued horses needed help, and though he wasn't a rehab expert, he'd dealt with some challenging steeds a time or two. And he knew how it felt to be hurt by those you were supposed to trust.

But he also knew the sting of knowing he'd played a role in someone else's pain. He couldn't undo what had happened to Bella any more than he could go back and keep the floodwaters from sweeping across Wyoming. But he could do good now.

They got back in the car, and a plume of dust followed them as they made their way toward a large stable barn east of two adjacent paddocks separated by a strip of grass. A group of hens pecked at the rocky ground, and a goat gnawed at a nearby fence post.

"This is where we keep many of our boarders and lesson horses." She shifted to Park and cut the engine. "We've got fifteen stalls and an indoor arena."

Moments later, their boots clonked on the cement aisle as they entered the stables, the scent of hay mixing with fresh earth, leather and horse. "You'll be spending most of your time here. We average just shy of fifteen lessons a week, but I'd really love for you to drum up more. Maybe even find a way to gain back some of the clients we've lost."

Interesting. Had something driven folks away? And had they left before or after Rheanna took over.

As they continued past the stalls, she paused periodically to offer a few of the horses peppermints. "We've got three tack rooms, one for students, one for staff and one for boarders." She stopped in front of a disorganized barn office. "The computer's older than a stegosaurus, but it works. You've also got a minifridge and microwave, plus we've got a full-size fridge to the right of the main entrance. Though, like I mentioned previously, you're welcome to eat breakfast and dinner at the house."

"I share this space with Bill?"

She nodded, then led him back outside and onto a dirt road dissecting more fenced pastureland. "We've got 200 acres, give or take, about one quarter of it forest. You remember my uncle did trail rides?"

He nodded.

"Far's I can tell, he quit doing that some time ago. I'd like to clean the trails up, so we can take people out on them again. Host birthday parties, bonfires, that sort of thing."

He raised an eyebrow. "Sounds like a lot of work."

She studied him for a moment. "How long did you say you planned to stay?"

He hadn't figured that out yet. "Long enough to make sure you and those horses you took in are able to stand."

The flicker of hope in her eyes reminded him of why a man should never make promises he might lack the power to keep. The fact that he felt such an urge not to let her down worried him even more.

Early the next morning, Rheanna scurried around the kitchen, trying to get breakfast made for whatever staff wandered in. The fact that T-Bone seemed to always be underfoot, hoping to catch food droppings, wasn't helping. Nor that Ivy had covered nearly every counter with baking supplies.

"What is all this for anyway?" Rheanna added a quarter of a cup of milk to a bowl of eggs, scrambled them, then poured them into a heated pan greased with previously reserved bacon drippings.

Ivy looked at her as if she'd gone daft. "I'm making paleo bars. It's what I do."

"Yes, I know. But did you get more orders? This seems like a lot for the Sweet Spot."

"I'm going to be hitting as many grocery stores, diners and coffee shops throughout the county as possible today to see if I can't secure some clients, or at least increase name recognition."

Rheanna frowned. That sounded expensive. "Make sure to return the car with a full tank."

Ivy still needed to pay her back for the last time she'd purchased gas, along with some grocery items Rheanna had picked up for her.

The television came on in the living room, and she poked her head out. Amelia lay sprawled on the couch, still in her pajamas. Rheanna marched toward her, grabbed the remote and flicked the cartoons off. "Uh-uh. You go get ready, now."

She pouted. "But I don't want to go to school."

"I've told you, it's not school. It's Vacation Bible School, and it'll be fun." Hopefully it would help her form relationships before fall, so she wouldn't feel so much like the newbie. Or get teased like she had back in Michigan. "You'll make friends, learn really cool stuff, and before you know it, the day will be over."

"What if no one likes me?" Her eyes teared up.

Rheanna's heart sank at remembering the difficulties Amelia had experienced back at her old school. An older kid had singled her out and started making fun of her. Soon, a handful of others joined in, causing Amelia to come home crying more often than not. When Rheanna tried talking to her teachers, that had only made things worse.

With a sigh, she plopped down beside her daughter, draped an arm over her shoulder and pulled her close. "Everyone will love you. You're smart, funny and have the coolest glittery shoes that light up whenever you walk, not to mention a backpack to match."

"And don't forget the fancy gel pens." Ivy entered wearing her bright, polka-dot apron and a dusting of some type of flour, likely coconut. "I've got an idea." She snapped her fingers, dashed toward the wall desk, rummaged around and returned with a blank sheet of printer paper. "This is a game we used to play when I was your age." She started folding the sheet into a pyramid shape.

Rheanna caught her friend's eye and mouthed thank you, then headed back into the kitchen. For all the frustration and expense Ivy had been causing lately, she had her good moments, like this morning. She was great with Amelia.

Rheanna needed to give her friend more grace. She'd been in such a rough place, prior to moving here. When Ivy lost the job she loved, she'd slipped into a worrisome depression. Rheanna understood all too well the grief that came with such a life-defining loss. She'd wanted to show Ivy the same support her friend had given her during her divorce but hadn't known how. Then she learned of her inheritance. This ranch seemed like the change they both needed.

The doorbell rang, and she hurried to answer it.

"Got it." Her mind instantly jumped to Dave, and her stomach gave an unwelcome flutter. Pausing to check her reflection in the mirror, she fluffed her hair, took a deep breath and opened the door.

The Dillard boys, three homeschooling teens she'd recently hired to help her make the ranch look more presentable, stood on her stoop wearing near identical ball caps and grins.

She suppressed a sigh and, gazing toward Bill's and Dave's cabins off on the horizon, chastised herself for her disappointment. She got over Dave years ago, so why was she so anxious to see him?

Because she was being foolish, that's why. She needed to wisen up before that man broke her heart for a second time.

She faced the boys with a smile. "Good morning, fellas. Breakfast will be ready soon." She moved aside to let them in.

She started to close the door behind them when she caught a glimpse of Bill approaching. She'd left messages on his and Dave's phones the night before, asking them to come talk to her first thing this morning. Hopefully those two would hit it off. Bill could get feisty when he felt like someone was stepping onto his turf, though he had to know this place, and therefore his job, wouldn't survive without competent help.

She told the boys to grab themselves a muffin and some orange juice, once again nagged Amelia to get dressed, then went outside to wait in the porch rocker.

The sun was just starting to peek over the horizon. Golden rays filtered through the distant trees and reflected off wispy clouds in gradient hues of pink and purple. After a light midnight rain, the air smelled earthy and fresh, and the decreased humidity seemed to have lowered the temperature some.

Upon reaching the house, Bill tipped his hat at her. "Ma'am." He climbed the steps, his boots clomping on the weatherworn wood. "You wanted to see me?"

"I did." She smiled and motioned for him to sit. "Can I grab you some coffee?"

He settled into the adjacent rocker, removed his hat and rested it on his knee. "Thank you. But no rush."

While he presented with all the manners of a Southern country boy, something about him challenged her trust. Not that she could afford to distrust him, considering this place would fail without him.

At least Dave was here now. Having owned his own ranch, he'd know how to keep this one afloat. But could he care for the rescues *and* manage their riding lessons? And for how long?

"Give me a minute." Footsteps crunched on gravel, and she glanced up to see Dave approaching in blue jeans, cowboy boots and his Stetson, and looking much too handsome. The sunrise framed his muscular build, casting an elongated shadow in front of him. Drawing near, he nodded first to her then to Bill. "Morning."

"I was just about to grab us some coffee." Why did she feel jittery all of the sudden? She hadn't behaved this way since…since the afternoon a much younger Dave Brewster stood on this porch, hat in hand, inviting her to Wilma's for fries and a shake. After a summer of trail rides and long walks, that had been their first official date.

Shaking off the memory and about a thousand that followed, she moved to the door and opened it. "You drink yours black?"

"Yes, ma'am." He took a deep breath, and his brow furrowed, his gaze extending beyond her.

She inhaled. Was that…?

The eggs! They were burning! All two dozen of them.

"Excuse me." She hurried inside to find smoke and steam billowing from the sink where the three Dillard boys stood.

She dashed over and peered at the charcoaled mess. "Sorry. But at least there's still—the bacon!"

Unfortunately, that was burned, too, leaving nothing but fruit and Ivy's dairy-and-gluten-free muffins. "I'll make more in a minute. In the meantime, have one of these." She handed one of the boys the plate of muffins and started to leave. Halfway through the living room, she turned back around for the coffee she'd promised both men.

By the time she returned to the porch with three steaming mugs, two in one hand, she felt more than a little flustered. "Sorry about that." She handed each man their cup, pulled a third rocker over and motioned for Dave to take it. Sitting herself, she addressed Bill first and told him about the rescues.

His frown deepened. "You can't be serious."

The edge in his voice didn't entirely surprise her. He was the definition of a crusty old rancher. No doubt he and her uncle had gotten along well. "What choice did I have?"

He scoffed. "Oh, I don't know. Let someone else take them?"

Dave set his mug on the small, circular table to his left. "Those men called everyone they could think of. No one had room."

Because all the other stable owners managed to keep their stalls filled? How many boarders had left her place to go somewhere else? Considering how far their numbers had fallen, based on what the books showed—a lot.

Somehow she needed to figure out a way to get those customers back.

Bill eyed Dave. "Who is this fella?"

Rheanna took in a deep breath and straightened. "That was the other thing I wanted to talk to you about. Dave, meet Bill, the ranch manager. Bill, meet Dave, our new riding instructor. He'll be helping train the foals, too, as he has time."

Based on the way Bill sized Dave up, Rheanna might've worried the two would come to blows. But though Dave maintained eye contact, his expression appeared tension free. Maybe even amused.

"He'll also be helping rehab the rescues," she said.

Bill shot a hard gaze between them. "Let me get this straight. Not only will we be pouring time and energy into over a dozen horses who might not survive past week's end. But you're going to use paid hours to do so?"

She shook her head. "In regard to the rescues, he'll be volunteering his time." Whatever he earned from lessons aside, she felt bad asking him to help for free, but she simply didn't have the funds to pay him. She wasn't entirely sure how she'd cover his training fees. "Hopefully the horse community will help with vet bills and such."

"Which reminds me..." Dave wiggled his phone from his back pocket. "I'll shoot my buddy Noah Williams a text, see if he can't help us figure out the steps to starting a nonprofit."

Bill's eyebrows shot up. "You mean you're planning on making this a thing?"

She crossed her arms. "Seems to me, being a rancher and all, you should want us doing all we can to see these horses stay alive."

He huffed. "If only the world were so simple." He stood. "You want to jeopardize the ranch your uncle poured his heart and soul into?" He raised his hands, palms out, and shook his head. "I've got work to do."

The porch jostled as he stomped down the steps and toward the east stables.

"Well, that's one less place at the breakfast table this morning." She shifted toward Dave, and his gentle, encouraging smile instantly soothed her. "You hungry? I've got a bunch of burnt bacon and healthy muffins waiting in the kitchen."

He laughed. "Burnt and healthy? Now what horseman in his right mind would decline a meal like that?"

His gentle teasing created a dull ache as memories surfaced of lazy summer afternoons filled with similar lighthearted banter.

How easy would it be for them to pick up where they left off?

But to what end? He'd left her once before. No doubt he'd do so again. Only this time, she had her daughter to think of. She had no intention of allowing herself to become involved with a man—any man—unless she knew, with certainty, he was the staying kind.

Chapter Five

Dave stopped into the stable office to check the lesson schedule. His first student wouldn't arrive until after noon, which gave him all morning to make calls and work with the rescued horses.

Actually, his entire week was pretty open, indicating Rheanna's ranch was worse off than he'd thought. He needed to figure out how to get more students coming in. That would be challenging, considering most folks in the local horse community would consider him an outsider.

Difficult but not impossible. He'd built his ranch from nothing, and largely as a Wyoming newbie. No reason he couldn't do something similar here.

He rummaged through dusty binders stacked on a partially caving shelf, on the floor, and on the long narrow and cluttered desk until he found old contacts. From the looks of it, this place used to be thriving. What had made the students leave and kept new ones from coming in?

Only one way to find out. He began making calls, starting at the year 2018. After about twenty minutes, he finally reached a live person.

He introduced himself in relation to Rheanna's ranch. "We're trying to improve our effectiveness and would love your feedback." Hopefully stating things that way would feel less like a sales pitch. "I noticed it's been a while since you've lessoned with us. May I ask why?"

"I loved it out there when you had Jesse on staff. After he left, everything went downhill, and y'all never seemed to hire quality instructors. I understand Emmitt's mind started slipping, and I'm sure that affected staffing. But I couldn't justify spending money on lessons that weren't doing me much good. When I know more than my instructor, there's a problem. Not to mention the last guy you had on had the temper of a wild boar."

Great. So the place had developed a bad reputation. He'd worried that might be the case. "I'm sorry for the frustration you experienced while still with us. I can understand why you left. I want to assure you that we've made a lot of changes."

Could he honestly say that? Now that he was running things, yes. And after he left? Well, hopefully Rheanna would find someone to continue whatever he started.

"We'd love the chance to re-earn your trust. How about if I offered you three free lessons? No obligations."

She paused. "I guess that'd be all right."

"Awesome. When would you like to come in?" He suggested some open slots, not wanting her to know how vacant his schedule truly was. Once they set a date and time, he called the next number in the notebook. By the end of the hour, he had three former students returning for trial lessons and had left messages with many others.

What was Rheanna's web presence like? He did an internet search for the ranch's name. It didn't pop up until the fourth page because whoever had set up the account had used some odd generic name for their website. So basically, few if any riders would find their site unless they typed in the exact URL. Not helpful.

He made himself a note to check web marketing prices. Then he clicked on the ranch website and skimmed through a few pages. Everything looked relatively up-to-date, which was good, though she could utilize training videos more. Unfortunately, her show schedule page hadn't been updated in over a year. Because she and her students no longer attended any?

"You get what you need?" A deep voice spoke from behind him.

He glanced back to see Bill eyeing him with an almost territorial scowl.

"Yep." He tore off his sheet of paper, filled about halfway down with notes.

Bill continued to watch him as he exited the office, his expression never softening. Did Dave make the man feel challenged or threatened? Did the guy have a thing for Rheanna? Only that wasn't the vibe Dave received, back when the three of them were talking on the porch. More likely he was just one of those angry old ranchers who didn't take kindly to newcomers.

Or had whatever garbage Rheanna's uncle spread about Dave and his family somehow made its way to the ranch manager? It didn't matter. Dave was here to save malnourished and abused horses, not to make friends.

How did Rheanna feel? He wished he didn't care, but truth was he did.

His phone rang, and he checked the return number. His friend in Cheyenne. He answered. "Mitch, buddy. What's going on?"

"Nothing bad. Actually, I might have good news. Or at least, something for you to chew on."

"Okay?"

"Folks are still underwater out here, literally and financially. The property next to mine is for sale, and my stock has grown considerably since the flood. I'm not looking to capitalize on anyone's loss or anything. But I need to make the best of what I've got. Way things are going, I expect at least twenty foals needing training come spring."

"Why do I sense a sales pitch coming?"

His friend laughed. "More like a new hire package."

He straightened. "What do you mean?"

"I could use a competent trainer. One with grit and integrity."

"Look, I appreciate the offer." He knew his friend only had the best of intentions. "But I've worked long and—"

"I meant as my partner."

Dave paused. "Partner?"

"Like I said, I'm managing more than I can handle. I need someone to help me run this place."

Business partners. Did ranchers even do that? Made sense. Mitch had the land and the stock. Dave had training experience but no usable property, at least not at the moment. But neither did he intend to sell his ranch. "What about my place?"

"Figure it's close enough you can still keep a handle on it."

"Run two places, you mean?" That sounded like more work than Dave could manage, no matter the financial payoff.

"I was thinking more like you and I working together in our areas of proficiency. Think of it as combining our strengths. I'd focus on breeding and sales. You could focus on training."

"Where is this coming from?" If Mitch was offering charity, while Dave could appreciate the heart behind it, he wasn't interested.

"My herd's doubled. Both Johnson and Williams decided they'd had enough of ranching and sold me their stock. I figured I could hire ranch hands who may or may not give a lick. Or I could go into business with a man I trust. The best trainer around."

Dave rubbed the back of his neck. "This is a lot to think about, bro. I'm honored you'd ask."

"You'd be doing me a favor."

"When do you need a decision?" What about Rheanna and sweet little Amelia?

"Ah, yesterday?" He chuckled. "How much time do you need?"

"Two weeks?"

"Honestly, I was hoping you'd jump on this. But I know that's not fair to ask. Two weeks works."

Call over, he remained standing in the office, rehashing it all. This could be an answer to prayer. If Rheanna could find someone to take his place here. She knew he didn't plan to stay long-term.

But if he left again, said goodbye to Rheanna, he had a feeling it'd be for good. His chest ached at the thought.

With a sigh, he drove a four-wheeler the quarter of a mile to where Rheanna kept the rescues. Though he'd stopped in to check on them the night before, he entered the barn with apprehension, not knowing what he'd find. It didn't take a vet degree to know those horses could die anytime, especially in the beginning. At least none of them had lost their ability to stand. Lack of mobility was practically a death sentence for a horse.

He entered the stables to find the vet working with a bony Friesian paint mix. The older gentleman was tall and olive-complected with black hair that brushed the top of his shirt collar. He and Dave had met briefly during the rescue mission but hadn't had much time to talk.

"Good morning." Dave stepped into the opened stall.

Dr. Wallow turned to face him, and the two men shook hands. "Brewster. Good to see you."

"How's the little lady holding up?" The black-and-white splotched mare was thinner than most of the others and stood with a drooping head and dull eyes.

"She's dangerously malnourished, and not just because she wasn't fed properly. I don't know when her teeth were last floated, if ever. Her tongue and cheeks are raw. Poor girl's probably become terrified to eat."

He winced. Horses' teeth grew throughout their lives, getting worn down as they ground their food. But because they often chewed unevenly, all sorts of problems arose, including the formation of sharp hooks and points that made eating excruciating.

Dave swallowed against a wave of emotion that threatened to make him ill. How could folks be so cruel? "I hope they prosecute the guy responsible for this."

A tendon in Dr. Wallow's cheek twitched, indicating he was fighting the same anger as Dave. "I plan to float all the other horses' teeth right away, but I'm not sure this sweet gal is stable enough for sedation. You giving her a mash?"

"Yeah. Beet pulp, rice bran, some senior feed, with about a handful of vitamins, all soaked in boiling water."

"Good. How much do you have on hand?"

"Thanks to donations from Sage Creek folks—" and the fact that the horses couldn't handle much food just yet "—I figure we've got enough to last the week."

"And after?"

He released a breath. "We get to praying." Something he imagined they'd all been doing since they first encountered those poor creatures. Dave didn't have the courage to ask the follow-up question—how long would Dr. Wallow keep treating these animals for free? Though h doubt the man wanted to continue doing so for as long as they needed, Dave also recognized the cost involved with feeding a family and running a veterinary clinic.

And so, he kept his question to himself. Not knowing the answer allowed him to retain hope that they both could stay as long as necessary. But the truth was, everyone involved had bills to pay.

After Dr. Wallow left, Dave spent the rest of his morning checking on the other horses, speaking softly to them and petting those that let him. Most of them acted pretty docile now, but there was no telling how they'd respond once their energy returned, nor how many could be retrained.

"It's hard to understand, isn't it, how people can be so heartless?"

He turned to find Rheanna leaning against the outer wall of an empty stall.

He nodded and walked toward her.

She rubbed her collarbone. "How will they heal from this?"

He'd heard his mom ask his social worker that same question about him, back when he'd first been placed with her and his father. His answer to Rheanna was the same as Angela Miller gave his parents, nearly two decades ago. "With a lot of love and time. Although you've got to know some of them might not recover. They might carry a fear of people for the rest of their lives."

"Then how will we ever find someone to adopt them?" Tiny lines formed on her delicate brow.

"...ve you given more thought to filing for nonprofit

...a visible breath. "Some. Honestly, it all feels ...ning. But let me know what I'd need to do."

...the weight on his chest feeling about fifty

pounds lighter. That was the first step to getting grant money funneled in. Then, maybe they could hire a full, well-qualified staff.

And he could return to his flooded ranch, start rebuilding and maybe even partner with his buddy.

And never see Rheanna again? If he stayed, he'd lose his ranch and potentially the business opportunity of a lifetime.

If he left, he'd lose any chance of rekindling what he and Rheanna once had.

A relationship she clearly had no interest in resuming, which was why he needed to remain focused on the reason he was here. To save those horses while tackling the never-ending paperwork related to the flood back home. He'd keep stepping until his boot hit a concrete barrier, and then he'd bring out a sledgehammer.

Watching the storm of emotions play out in her eyes, he longed to grab her hand and pull her close. But their relationship didn't allow for that. Not anymore.

She gazed down the stable aisle. "I'm not saying that'll work, or even that it's a viable option. Just that I'll consider it."

"I understand." Yet, the hope in her eyes suggested she wasn't any more ready to give up on these horses than he was.

Her phone chimed a text, and she glanced at the screen and sighed.

"Everything all right?" Probably wasn't his business to ask.

"Amelia's at Trinity Faith's Vacation Bible School this week. She developed a feverless stomachache and wants to come home."

"Ah. I had a few of those when I was her age." More than a few. Seemed his insides had been tied up in knots from the time he could remember until midway through his sophomore year—once he realized his last home placement would indeed be his last. "You need to go pick her up?"

"That is most assuredly what I should not do, though I want to." She shared Amelia's growing social anxiety and explained how she was trying to help her conquer it prior to the new school year. "It doesn't help that she was bullied quite a bit at her old elementary. I tried talking to her teacher, the principal, even the school counselor. They promised to address the situation. I'm sure they tried, but less than a week later, she came home in tears telling me about the same old issues."

"Kids can be so mean."

"I'm just hoping things will be different here."

He sensed she was talking about more than just her daughter and was half tempted to ask her about that. But then she straightened and grabbed a rake resting on the exterior wall of the adjacent stall. "I should probably stop talking and get working."

"I'll help."

"Thanks." Her smile, though tinged with fatigue, reminded him of all the summer afternoons they'd spent together, sometimes lazing around, talking about nonsensical dreams for their futures. Other times, mucking stalls, like they were about to do this morning.

If someone had asked him a week ago about those moments, or about Rheanna in general, he would've said he'd long since moved on. Standing here now, seeing her vulnerability, her compassion for the horses, her love for her daughter—in short, seeing the girl he fell in love with peek through, he wasn't so sure.

He worried if they kept working side by side, once it

came time to leave, he'd be walking away from Sage Creek in the same condition he had last time—heartbroken.

He grabbed a nearby wheelbarrow. "How about I tackle the dirty work?" He grinned at his play on words. "While you mix up their morning mash?"

Distance. So long as he kept his distance, everything would work out fine.

What's more, the sooner he helped her turn this place into a thriving nonprofit, the sooner he could return home to his less emotionally confusing life.

Rheanna spent the rest of the morning feeding the rescues a mash the vet prescribed. Every once in a while, Dave popped his head into the stall. He'd eyed the water bucket and food, gave her an encouraging nod and moved on to his next chore. Their working together felt like old times, and her heart didn't seem any more resistant to his charm than when they'd been kids.

Only now she fully intended to let her head lead. Because whoever said it was better to have loved and lost had never sobbed their way through half a gallon of ice cream.

By noon, when his first riding student arrived, he'd started organizing an overly cluttered tack and long-neglected tack room. "I'll finish this later." He exited and closed the door securely. "In the meantime, let's keep this shut so no disease-carrying critters find their way in and contaminate the feed."

She nodded, took some time to finish sweeping the aisle, then meandered back toward the house to make a few phone calls. On the way, she stopped in to the arena to watch Dave, noting the firm set of his jaw as he gave his student his full attention. The gentle encouragement he offered and careful instruction.

He clearly knew what he was doing. Within twenty

minutes, he'd taught Mrs. Johnson, a notoriously nervous rider who tended to death-grip the reins, to rely on her legs and seat. What's more, she actually looked relaxed. Like she was enjoying herself even.

If he kept this up and word of mouth got out… Maybe Rheanna could save this ranch after all.

Except Dave wasn't planning on staying. The ache the thought triggered suggested her heart was trying to hold her head captive.

She gave herself a mental shake and thought through her to-do list. Her next big task? Getting the grounds' trail riding ready. The work was more labor intensive than anything, which meant she could likely hire high school students. But even that could get expensive.

After picking Amelia up from her Vacation Bible School, Rheanna spent the rest of the afternoon calling around—the football coach, Trinity Faith's youth director, whomever might have an in with teens. By suppertime, she'd managed to secure about forty hours' worth of free labor from kids touched by the rescue operation and who wanted to help her mission in some way.

She told Ivy about her progress and her assessment of Dave's horsemanship skills.

"That's great." Ivy grabbed a bag of almond flour and poured it into a measuring cup. "Who knows. Maybe he'll stick around longer than you think."

Her pulse accelerated, and heat immediately flooded her cheeks. She cleared her throat and turned to the stove to hide what was likely an obvious blush. "Well, he's here for now, and we're making progress. That's what matters."

"Speaking of handsome, ranch-saving cowboys…" Ivy gazed out the kitchen window.

The doorbell rang a moment later.

"I'll get it," Amelia called out from the other room.

Soon, her chatter, punctuated by Dave's deep laughter, drifted toward the kitchen.

Rheanna poked her head into the living room, momentarily captivated by their sweet interaction.

"Miss Dainty Paws had kittens. I seen them today when I was feeding the chickens." Amelia practically bounced in her excitement. "She's the fat orange cat with the white splotch on her face. Well, she used to be fat. I didn't know that was on account of her babies. I asked Mom if I could have one as a pet, to keep inside and sleep with me at night and read stories to—do you think cats like to listen to stories, Mister Dave?"

"Don't see why not, especially if it's a story about milk and tuna." The skin around his eyes crinkled. He'd make a great father someday.

"Miss Ivy says animals are more intitive than we think?"

"Inta-what?"

Rheanna smiled. "Intuitive."

He nodded. "Ah. Bet she's right. Least, that's the case with horses. Did you know they can read facial expressions?"

Amelia cocked her head. "What does that mean?"

"They can tell how a person's feeling based on whether they're smiling or frowning or whatnot. There was even a horse that learned how to spell and answer math problems by watching his owner's face."

Amelia's eyes widened. "Really?"

"Yep." He went on to tell of a gelding named Jim Key who'd been owned by a former slave and self-taught veterinarian. "Folks called him the world's smartest horse. He and his trainer traveled the United States, from Atlanta to Chicago, wowing audiences with the animal's ability to 'read, write, and do simple sums.' Eventually folks

wanted to know the how-to of it all and started doing stud-
ies. Turned out the horse wasn't ready for the first grade,
after all. He'd simply learned facial clues."

Amelia grinned. "I want to do that. How can I do that?
Can you teach me?" She spun toward Rheanna. "Can you
take me to the library, Mama, so I can get some books?"

Rheanna checked the time on her phone. "It'll be closed
by the time we get there, sweetie."

"Then tomorrow? Before Bible school? And to the grocery, too, for paper? Then I can make flash cards like you
do for my spelling words."

"Come eat." Sharing an amused smile with Dave, Rheanna placed her hand to the back of Amelia's head and
guided her into the kitchen. "And as to all those errands,
assuming I'm back, yes. And I can't imagine I wouldn't
be."

"If you're not?"

"Sorry, sweetie, but I've got a doctor's appointment
in Houston, and Aunt Ivy's car's not fixed yet, so she
wouldn't be able to take you." Rheanna needed to talk
to Ivy about how she was handling her finances and set
clear boundaries regarding who paid for what when. The
fact that they'd entered this ranching/health-food venture
together certainly complicated things. What Ivy considered a business investment, one she swore she'd pay back
double, Rheanna was beginning to see as a drain.

Ivy halted midway to the table. "Wait. What's going
on?"

"Remember, you're watching Amelia so I can go to my
appointment in Houston?"

She placed a salad bowl and water pitcher with more
lemons than ice cubes on the table. "Sorry, but I've got
back-to-back meetings with prospective buyers in Austin. Which reminds me, I need to whip up a batch of keto

raspberry bars tonight. Maybe some double-fudge protein balls, as well. Can you reschedule?"

"It's too late for that. They'll charge me."

"Call one of the ladies from Trinity Faith's quilting club."

"I'm not comfortable doing that." She'd already asked the community for enough help as it was, and with caring for rescues, would have to do so plenty in the near future. She needed to save her SOS's for true emergencies. Ivy backing out of an agreement wasn't one of them.

"They'd love to help."

Rheanna crossed her arms. "We talked about this—before I even made the appointment."

"I'm sorry, but I completely forgot."

"That's not my problem."

Ivy sighed. "What do you want me to do? It's not like I can cancel all my meetings."

"I can help." Dave pulled out his phone and tapped on the screen a few times. "My first lesson isn't until three thirty."

Rheanna frowned. "I can't ask you to do that. Besides, we've only got one car between us." Then again, it was her car, and this was Ivy's error. She turned back to her friend. "I can drop you off at the rental in Brenham on my way to Houston."

"That's out of my way, not to mention that'll be expensive."

"It's not exactly on mine, either. But I'm willing to take a slight detour. Other than that, I don't know what to tell you."

Ivy huffed. "Fine."

Dave grinned. "Problem solved." He placed a hand on Amelia's shoulder. "Looks like you're hanging with me tomorrow, kiddo."

"Yay!" Amelia beamed and made a fist punch, and for a moment, Rheanna caught a glimpse of what a father-daughter relationship could be.

Every child deserved a daddy.

Chapter Six

The next morning, Dave spread all his flood-related papers onto the table, grateful he'd kept them stored in his truck. Prior to coming to Sage Creek, he'd thought of renting one of those private mailboxes at a shipping store to keep everything in.

Ultimately, he determined that'd be a pain, having to go there whenever he needed something, especially since he wasn't sure where he'd be staying from one day to the next. Since his stable office was as flooded as his house was, he'd kept everything important, including a treasure box filled with childhood mementos, with him in a carry-on suitcase.

Seemed a man needed a math and legal degree to figure all this stuff out. Unfortunately, he didn't have flood insurance, but his farm equipment would be covered. Minus his deductible. If only he hadn't opted for the cheaper plan.

At least his bills were paid through the month's end.

Some of his buddies were already talking about filing Chapter 12 bankruptcy. Dave refused to entertain that option.

He glanced at the time on the microwave. He needed to

get a move on if he wanted to finish his morning chores in time to take Amelia to day camp.

Heading out, he smiled to himself, remembering the little girl's wide-eyed look when he'd told her about the horse who could "spell." She'd peppered him with questions all dinner long. *Could all horses read faces? Sad and angry and happy faces? And what if you did this?* Then she'd shown him about half a dozen different and exaggerated expressions.

And now she wanted to find books and make flash cards. He laughed. That'd keep her busy for a while. That kid sure was a cutie, and like her mom, much too liable to capture his heart if he wasn't careful. Her sweet and curious nature awakened longings for a family he'd fought hard to suppress after his failed engagement.

He drove a ranch four-wheeler to the quarantine stables to ensure the rescues were fed and watered. Starting tomorrow, he'd increase their rations and decrease their feedings to three times a day. He paused outside the stall of the pregnant mare he'd named Asha, which meant hope. She still looked painfully skinny, but her eyes weren't so droopy, and once she saw him, they indeed seemed to spark with hope.

"Hey, there, pretty lady."

She eyed him with caution but eventually inched toward him. He slowly reached out, let her sniff him, then he moved to scratch her forehead. She flinched and pulled back.

He dropped his hand. "I won't hurt you, girl. Neither will anyone else ever again, if I have anything to say about it."

They needed to figure out some way to screen potential adopters. Make sure folks understood how to care for a horse, how to train with love and mutual respect rather than fear.

"How's that baby of yours? Kicking and moving around? Any thoughts on what we should name her? Or him."

As he kept talking, voice smooth and low, she continued to watch him and appeared to relax some.

"I'll stop back sometime this afternoon." The farrier was scheduled to come out after lunch. Though most of these horses had yet to recover their fight, the man would still need help. After that, Dave had an open house of sorts where he'd invited a local moms' group and their kids to come in for a free evening lesson. Hopefully some of them would turn into steady customers. Rheanna had given him the okay to run a social media ad tomorrow. That should help, too.

By the time he reached the house, Amelia and her mom were ready and waiting for him.

"She's got her Bible and verse pages in her backpack. I put offering money in an envelope."

"From my own piggy bank." Amelia grinned. "The money is for poor kids who can't buy their own school supplies."

He smiled. "That's mighty kind and grown-up of you."

Amelia beamed and stretched to her full height.

"I should probably go." Rheanna gave Amelia a hug, then held her at arm's length. "Now you be good for Mister Dave, you hear?"

The child bobbed her head, her long braids bouncing against her shoulders.

"Oh." Rheanna pulled a twenty-dollar bill from her back pocket. "This is for her…flash card supplies. In case I'm not back in time to take her."

He wanted to decline the payment, but the look in her

eyes told him doing so would prick her pride, which had been hurt enough the moment she asked for help.

How long had she been going it alone?

"She'll probably be ravenous after VBS." Rheanna grabbed her purse off the entryway accent table. "And will try to convince you that she normally eats cookies or ice cream or other sugary treats. But she has snacks in baggies in the fridge she can choose from."

He gave a quick nod and salute.

She laughed, then her expression turned more serious. "Thank you."

"No problem."

"No, I mean it. Really, thank you. I know this is a lot to ask, on top of everything else. I'm not sure what I would've done otherwise."

"We're going to have fun, aren't we, peanut?" He smoothed a hand over Amelia's head, his heart warming when a grin lit the child's eyes and face. As if the thought of spending time with him brought her joy. He'd sure miss that girl once he left.

"Yep! I can show you my art supplies, if you want. And Cuddles and Chocolate Chip and Rainbow."

He shot an inquisitive look to Rheanna, who stood with one hand on the doorknob. "Her stuffed animal collection."

"Ah." He smiled. "Sounds like a plan."

"If I'm not back by then." Rheanna stepped onto the porch, the morning sun framing her. "And that's a big if."

With a wave, she cast a glance at Ivy, who scurried about shoving things into one of her massive totes, then descended the stairs. A moment later, Ivy followed her out. Soon the sound of pebbles crunching beneath tires faded.

He and Amelia still had time to kill before he needed to take her to the church, so he let her give him a tour of her room. This led to her showing him every "diary," sketch-book, trinket and toy she owned, including her massive stuffed animal collection.

The girl had to have at least fifty critters stacked on her bed, under it, on her closet shelf and in a hammock-like thing draped in the east corner of her room. They all had names, and she could remember when and from whom she had received each one.

"Your love language must be gifts."

Amelia scrunched her nose. "My what?"

"How you give and…" She wouldn't understand all that psychobabble. "It makes you feel special, when people give you something, big or small."

"Yeah, like when Mama bought me this backpack. We weren't even shopping for me, but I saw it and loved it and showed it to her. I didn't even ask her if she'd buy it, on account of I knew she didn't have a lot of money that day. Or ever."

She frowned and dropped her gaze, but then her grin returned. "But she knew how much I liked it so she bought it for me anyway. Gave it to me as a surprise, so I'd have something new when I started school." She huffed. "I don't want to go to school. I don't like it."

He gave her a sideways hug. "Being the new girl is tough."

"Yeah. But I made a friend. At VBS."

"You did?"

She nodded. "Her name is Annie, and she likes draw-ing and singing and animals, just like me. I told her she could come to the barn and ride one of the horses. But not the broken ones, right?"

The broken ones. A sad but fitting description. For now. "Not yet, but maybe once they're feeling better."

"I heard that man with the gray hair and big belly say

no one wanted them. Is that true? That no one wanted those horses? Except Mama did, and so did you. Right, Mister Dave?"

He swallowed, the sadness, almost desperation, in her eyes tugging at his heart. It had to be hard for her little mind to process, seeing those horses in such a state. How would she respond if any of them died? "I do."

She grinned. "I knew you did. Can we tell them?"

He wrinkled his brow. "Tell them what, pumpkin?"

"That we want them? So they aren't so sad."

"If you want."

She gave one brisk nod, then darted to her pink-and-purple vanity standing along the opposite wall. She grabbed a glittery headband, put it on and stared at her reflection. "My daddy didn't want me, either. But my mama said that was just because he didn't have enough love in his heart for other people. Not for her, either." She turned to him and smiled. "Do you like my hair?"

Tears pricked his eyes, and a sudden urge to pull that precious child close, to hug all her hurts away, swept over him. "You're beautiful."

His phone rang, and he glanced at the screen. Ivy? Why was she calling? He answered. "Ma'am? What can I do you out of?"

"Hi. I'm so sorry to bother you, but I'm kind of in a bind. I'm in Brenham picking up my rental. I have a meeting in Austin in just under two hours and don't have time to swing back home. Only I left all my addresses at the house."

"Okay. I'm here now."

"Great! I think I left them with a bunch of my notes on the built-in desk next to the kitchen. If you wouldn't mind taking pictures of all of it. They should be together."

He exited the room and continued down the hall to an

overflowing stacks of papers. "What do they look like?" He sifted through a pile of unopened mail, old invoices, a grocery and to-do list...

"They should have Austin addresses and information on bakeries, diners and cafés on them. Along with the names of owners and notes on whether I called them, when and if we scheduled a meeting."

He continued searching. Those ladies needed a personal secretary, especially if they were going to turn the ranch into a nonprofit. Amid a pile of mail, a legal envelope with the word *Urgent* stamped on it caught his eye. It was from the IRS. He checked the postage date. Two months ago. Not good, and based on everything scattered before him and all he'd seen piling up in the barn office, these ladies had probably made some filing errors.

He needed to tell Rheanna.

Hopefully she could easily rectify whatever warranted the letter. Unfortunately, his gut told him this was serious.

Rheanna returned home feeling equally exhausted and encouraged. She sat in her car, engine off, to give herself a moment to regroup. Every doctor's appointment always triggered anxiety and memories of that awful year when everything, including life itself, felt uncertain. She knew, logically, she was fine. Her lifelong follow-ups were just that—follow-ups. The chance of her developing any of the complications health professionals were required to mention were minimal. But just knowing the *C* word was a possibility provoked feelings of vulnerability.

She closed her eyes against the memory of when that disease first became personal.

She'd made it through and was here now—with a daughter to raise and a ranch to run. With a deep breath, she exited her car and was immediately accosted by the heat and humidity characteristic of the Texas Hill country. She wasn't looking forward to working outside this afternoon.

Climbing the porch steps, she glanced at the time on her phone. Just after one, thanks to a majorly delayed appointment followed by an accident-caused standstill on the freeway. Starved, she dashed inside to eat and change her clothes, then headed to the indoor arena in search of Dave. She found him in the middle of a lesson with Paige Gilbertson, the Chicago journalist turned local murder mystery writer.

Standing in the center of the arena, Dave rotated, holding the lead rope, as Poppie, one of their older lesson horses, walked in a circle. "Nice job. Shoulders back, and remember to keep your eyes ahead. Like I said, a horse trots with a two-beat gait. You want to rise with Poppie's rhythm. Now, up, one-two, one-two." His steady count signaled to Paige when to lift and touch back, lightly, to her saddle. "Perfect."

He caught Rheanna's gaze, and a slight smile, almost as if he was happy to see her, lit his face. He nodded hello, then refocused on Paige. "Oops. You're rising on the inside leg. To fix that, sit for two beats then start again."

Paige did as instructed.

"How's that feel?" He rotated as she circled the arena.

Paige half laughed, half huffed. "Not as terrifying as when I first got on."

"That's progress."

Rheanna thought back to when Dave had worked with her, the city girl who hadn't known an English saddle from a Western.

Practically raised on the animals, he connected with them in a way she hadn't understood. He'd made it his mission to bring her into his world. He'd been so patient, so gentle—and quick to offer that boyish grin that always accelerated her pulse.

What a summer that had been. The summer she'd first fallen in love.

Dave guided the horse to a stop, and Paige glanced in Rheanna's direction with a grin. "Hi."

Rheanna walked out to them. "Never thought I'd see you riding."

Dave helped Paige down. She scratched Poppie's neck, and the horse leaned his face toward her. "Figured, living in horse country, I needed to tackle my silly fear once and for all."

"Well, you're in good hands." Her gaze shot to Dave, and his eyes held hers for a moment. Heat flushed her face. Clearing her throat, she looked away. "So, how's the dinner theater?"

"Doing well! We're finally seeing fruit from all our rebranding."

"I should talk to you and Jed about that—rebranding, I mean." Rheanna suppressed a sigh.

"Stop by anytime." Paige removed her riding helmet. "Speaking of time, I need to get cleaned up for work. We've got a private party this evening, a doctor's office from La Grange."

"Fun," Rheanna said.

"And lucrative." Paige tucked her helmet under her arm and fluffed her hair. "You know, y'all should maybe do something like that. Promote team-building opportunities to local businesses."

Rheanna scraped her teeth across her bottom lip. "Like a group lesson you mean?" That sounded like nothing short of organized chaos.

Paige shrugged. "That or maybe trail rides or something."

"It's an idea." But first she had to get their trails cleaned up. That was a hefty task in itself.

The three of them walked Poppie back to her stall, where they chatted a bit more before sending Paige off with a time and day to return for her second lesson.

Rheanna followed Dave into the stable office. "How'd things go today?"

"Great. And you?"

"Fine."

He wrote in the paper calendar on his desk, then straightened. "Amelia and I arrived at the church early, so she introduced me to all the volunteers."

Rheanna raised her eyebrows. "All of them?"

He laughed. "Pretty much. Course, I already knew most of them, but I didn't tell her that."

Instead, he let her have her moment. Insightful and sweet. "Sounds like she kept you busy." Clearly, he'd made quite the impression on her, so much so that she wanted to share her world with him. Which meant she was becoming attached.

How would she feel when it came time for Dave to leave?

"That she did." He paused, and his gaze intensified. "Listen, I wasn't trying to snoop or anything, but Ivy called me this morning asking me to find something for her." He went on to tell her about a letter he'd found in a stack of envelopes, likely grabbed from the mailbox, then deposited without a second glance—or mention.

"From the IRS?" Her stomach felt queasy. "What would they want?"

"I'm sure it's nothing to be concerned about. I left it on your desk, on top of the other stuff."

She really needed to work on organization. Who knew what else she had lying in that ever-growing pile? She also needed to talk to Ivy about paying attention to their mail, or better yet, letting Rheanna pick it up.

She rubbed her temple. "I'll take a look."

"Want me to come? I'm no expert by any means, but I have some experience handling the business side of ranching."

She studied him. Seemed she was relying on him more and more, which only increased her anxiety when she thought about his upcoming departure. "I… When's your next class?"

"Had a cancelation." He glanced at his phone screen. "I've got about an hour and a half."

"Maybe we can talk about nonprofit stuff? I had an idea I wanted to run by you, as well."

"Throw in an iced lemonade, and I'm all yours."

His easy smile helped put her at ease. And drew her to him in a way she had no business entertaining. She hated how her emotions kept playing games with her rational side. She and Dave had ended things long ago. She had no intention of resurrecting something that had led to such heartache and likely would again.

Nor would she put sweet Amelia at risk of experiencing similar rejection.

Like her uncle had warned her numerous times, some men just didn't have it in them to stick around.

Dave accompanied Rheanna back to the house. "You said you have ideas to share?"

She nodded. "Have you ever been to a trail riding event like they have in West Virginia?"

"Never heard of them."

"Usually a local horse group hosts a two-to-three-day deal where people ride from a starting point to a campground. They come from all over, most of them with their own horses, though some 'rent.'" She made air quotes.

"They load their gear into vans that others drive to the site. Another group mans a large cookout. Vendors come and everything."

He scratched his jaw. "Might be easier than hosting a horse show. Don't need to worry about hiring judges and setting up show rules and standards and whatnot."

"A big riding event would still require a lot of know-how and legwork. And effective advertising to get registrations. But what we raise might make it worth it. We could have people pay to participate, but we might receive more if we asked for donations."

"True. People can be pretty generous when given the chance. Are there any laws or regulations we need to be aware of? Any permits we need to get?"

"I don't know." Was she prepared for all the hours of research she'd need to do to run an event well?

"How about I make some calls this evening and see if we can't get folks to help."

She felt the tension ease from her shoulders. "Thank you." His confident smile helped boost her hope. He always seemed to have that effect on her. And maybe if things were different for the both of them, they could pick up where they left off.

Right before he left.

Besides, she had a ranch to run, as did he, in an entirely different state, once he got his up and going again.

Deliciously cool air swept over her as she entered her house. "That lemonade sounds pretty good right about now." She held her door open for him. "I'll grab our drinks." She dashed into the kitchen and returned, glasses in hand, to find him surveying the living room.

She handed him his lemonade. "What is it?"

"Just...remembering, I guess." He shook his head.

"Thinking about how much things have changed, and how much has stayed the same."

"I haven't really had time to do much decorating." She knew he wasn't referring to the bare white walls she hadn't gotten around to painting or hanging photos on. But talking interior design felt easier. Safer.

She set her drink on a pile of papers to her right and slowly picked up the IRS envelope, dreading what might be inside.

He came over to her, started to place a hand on her shoulder, then dropped it to his side. "Everything okay?"

Her chest tightened as she read the letter. "The IRS is contesting some past claims and wants us to substantiate them. From two years ago."

"Were you even around then?"

She shook her head. Had her uncle lied on his taxes?

"Now what?" She rubbed at her collarbone. "I don't even know where all my uncle's records are." She flipped over the envelope so that the postage side faced up. "And I don't have much time."

"Won't Bill know? He's been managing this ranch long enough."

"Hopefully. I'll ask him."

Dave placed his hand on her shoulder.

"We'll get through this." He spoke with confidence, as if he intended to make good on that promise. "Together."

It took all her self-control not to fall into his embrace, to let him hold her in his strong arms like he used to when they were kids. Offering his strength in place of her weakness. Telling her everything would be all right and promising to stand beside her through whatever was causing her pain.

She placed her hand on his, and nodded. "Thank you."

The threat of tears pricked her eyes. She took a deep breath. "I better call Bill."

The sooner the better, because if she stood here much longer, feeling so vulnerable while Dave appeared so strong, so caring, her head would lose the battle over her heart.

And she couldn't let that happen. She couldn't love and lose Dave a second time.

Chapter Seven

Rheanna found Bill mending a fence on the far side of the east paddock. He cast her a sideways glance when she approached but remained focused on his work. "Hey."

She took a deep breath to calm her nerves. "Hi. Do you have a minute?"

He shifted to face her with one quick nod.

She told him about the letter she'd received. "You keep the files in the barn office, correct?"

Pulling on his ear, he studied her for a long moment. "Mostly, for this year anyway. But you're talking two years back, when your uncle's mind was first starting to go."

In other words, those records could be anywhere, or nonexistent. She'd heard stories of people with Alzheimer's placing random things, like car keys, in the fridge, and milk in the pantry. And while her uncle's mistakes had probably been accidental, she doubted the IRS would care.

Bill shucked off his work gloves. "Get me the list of what all they want, and I'll work on rounding it up."

"I appreciate that."

Unfortunately, every moment they spent untangling this tax mess stole their already limited man-hours for the ranch. Walking back to the house, she mentally listed all her responsibilities. The Dillard boys were stopping by this afternoon to help her start clearing out her trails. How much supervision would they need? Then there was the ranch entrance. Ivy still hadn't planted the flowers as she'd promised. She shot her a reminder text just as she pulled up to the house.

Apparently, she'd gotten her car back.

She stepped out and flashed Rheanna a smile. "I can pretty up the entrance no problem." She moved to the trunk and began unloading groceries. "Think you can give me a hand?"

"Sure." Rheanna needed to do something active, something to slow her swirling thoughts enough so she could figure out what to say and do. She peeked inside one of the paper bags. More almond flour? "I take it you got some orders?"

"A friend's hosting a free spa day for the moms in her church, with a cocoa bar and magazine-reading section. She asked if we'd donate some treats, said we could display our business cards—for our health food and the ranch. I figured it'd be a great way to get our name out."

"That sounds expensive."

"Like they say, you've got to spend money to make money." Ivy climbed the porch steps, the wood bowing slightly beneath her. "Which is why I wanted to talk."

Inside, Amelia was sprawled out on the floor, her markers and notepads in front of her.

Rheanna smiled. "Hey, there's my little artist. Don't forget to practice your memory verse."

She lifted her chin. "I already know it."

"Wow, impressive." The promise of candy was a great motivator, apparently. Chuckling to herself, Rheanna followed Ivy into the messy and cluttered kitchen—which resembled most of the rest of her house—and helped her unload groceries.

"I made a lot of great connections in Austin." Ivy placed a gallon of almond milk in the fridge. "Connections that led to connections and will lead to more connections. I really think we can get into the organic stores. I'm going to line up some meetings next week. Hopefully I can snag time from the bigwigs—the decision makers. But we need a loan to make it happen. We need to figure out a way to speed up production, lower our margins, that sort of thing."

Ivy had a tendency to let her enthusiasm overpower her logic.

"About that." Rheanna placed a bottle of vanilla in the cupboard and faced Ivy. "I support you, for sure...to a point. But I can't throw any more money into this." Especially considering, up until now, Ivy had brought in very little. "I have to focus on the ranch."

"What are you saying? That you're out?" She crossed her arms.

"We just need to be wise with our finances is all." Especially since they were now under IRS scrutiny. She told Ivy about the letter, and how they could potentially owe money on back taxes.

Ivy fumbled her way to a kitchen chair and sat. "What does that mean? Could they seize this place?"

Rheanna's stomach soured. She hadn't thought of that. "I don't know."

"People go to jail for that type of stuff."

"Only if they refuse to pay."

"But what if we don't have the money?"

"I don't know." Rheanna felt ill. This all was more than she knew how to deal with, more than her brain could handle. The ranch—with a surly and uncommunicative ranch hand and not nearly enough boarders. The rescued horses, which she might not be able to feed by month's end. Dave, whom she desperately needed to stay on, but who triggered emotions she'd thought she'd overcome and didn't have the courage to process.

And now this.

Ivy stood and came to her. "It'll be okay." She placed an arm around her shoulder. "I know it. After all you've overcome, this is nothing but a speed bump. God wouldn't move us here, then hang us out to dry."

Out to dry. Rheanna thought of Dave's property back in Wyoming, and where he was likely returning, as soon as all that floodwater receded.

Leaving her, just like he had over a decade ago.

"Show me the letter." Ivy tugged Rheanna toward her desk and pulled up an extra chair. She gently guided Rheanna to sit, then did the same.

Rheanna handed her the document.

Ivy read it. "Okay. So, we'll start with expenses. Where'd your uncle keep all his receipts?"

"Apparently, all over the place." Rheanna sighed and surveyed the piles of paper covering her desk. "Bill took over at some point, probably once it became clear my uncle was losing his ability to function. But I'm not sure when that was or for how long."

"You talked to him?"

She nodded. "He said he'd help. When he could, but he didn't seem thrilled with the idea." Not that she blamed him. He had a lot of responsibility, and an insufficient staff, as it was. "But I do have some stuff. I started sorting through things when we first moved here."

"I remember."

"Then I got overwhelmed with the ranch." She'd long said they needed a bookkeeper. Operating funds aside, she should've hired one on long ago. "Let me grab what I have." She dashed into her room and returned with an armload full of labeled shoeboxes, which she deposited on the floor.

Sitting cross-legged on the cool wood, Rheanna began going through bills and receipts one slip of paper at a time. T-Bone, who'd been lying in the sun streaming through the window, ambled over and plopped down beside her. He rested his head on her leg, almost as if trying to comfort her.

"You're such an intuitive creature." Rheanna scratched him behind his ears.

Meanwhile, Ivy made a list of each expense—the date, how much it was, and whether it'd been paid in cash, check or credit card.

Rheanna tossed some spam in the trash and revealed a sheet of paper with notes from her original business plan.

She huffed and showed it to Ivy. "Man, was I way off."

She'd severely underestimated the cost of feed and basic horse care and overestimated how many boarders they'd get in. They seriously needed to find a way to increase their profits—and make sure they documented every dollar carefully.

She told Ivy about her trail-riding event idea.

Ivy's eyes lit up. "That sounds like fun!"

"And a lot of work."

"So, we'll get help." She grabbed another sheet of paper from one of the shoeboxes and studied it briefly. "You know, that'd be a great place to sell our granola bars and power balls."

Rheanna stifled an eye roll. "How about we figure out how to get the IRS off our backs first?"

"Deal."

Someone knocked on the door. It opened to reveal Dave

standing on the stoop, the three homeschooled teens Rheanna had hired to help her clean up the trails gathered behind him.

Dave tipped his hat with a smile that nearly stole her breath.

"Ma'am." The boys nodded hello.

"Oh." Rheanna stood and hurried to greet them. She'd completely lost track of time. "Thanks for coming." She cast a glance to Ivy behind her. "Mind if we finish this later?"

Ivy shrugged. "Sure. I've got some baking to do anyway, though I'll work through this stuff a bit longer."

Rheanna smiled. "Thanks." For all her quirks and poor decision-making, Ivy could be a great friend when she wanted to be.

Rheanna stepped out into the muggy late-afternoon air and closed the door behind her. "You fellas ready to work?"

The teens smiled. "Yes, ma'am."

She turned to Dave. "I figured we'd check out the property to see what needs clearing and what not."

Dave rested his hand on his belt buckle. "Sounds like a plan." With a slight smile, he nudged one of the teens. "You boys handy with a machete?"

Their eyes lit up like he'd just offered them an all-expenses-paid amusement park vacation.

Hunter, the taller of the three, looked from Dave to his brothers then back to Dave. "We get to use one?"

He laughed. "Not sure what Ms. Stone has lined up for us."

"Hold on." She ran back inside, then returned with a stack of printed papers. "I just want you to scope out the trails for now. Note their condition, how wide they are, when the width changes, what kind of obstacles like roots and rocks might pose a tripping hazard, and what it'll take to make them rideable. Make sure branches aren't hanging too low."

She handed them each a clipboard with paper and a stubby pencil pulled from her pocket. "I printed out a checklist for you all. And please take pictures. You all got your phones?"

"Yes, ma'am," they said in unison.

Dave nodded and held his up.

She gazed toward the tree line. "Does that sound manageable?"

"Yes, ma'am." Hunter squeezed the brim of his ball cap. "We've helped our dad with stuff like this a lot of times."

"Perfect." She studied her map again, then looked at the boys. "How about you three start on the east end of the property."

"Yes, ma'am." They nodded and darted off toward their indoor arena.

Dave tucked his pencil behind his ear. "Want me to stick with you?"

She and Dave, walking the length of the property, just like old times. A flutter swept through her midsection as an image of the two of them, sitting beneath a gnarled old oak, shoulder to shoulder, resurfaced. She couldn't remember what had been going on that day, but something had frustrated her. Most likely, her uncle. Seemed he was always finding something to pick at. Dave had noticed she'd been upset and tried to tease a smile out of her. Stealing her heart one kind and gentle act at a time.

Somehow, they ended up under that old oak, the place where he'd kissed her for the first time. Man, had she loved him.

And now?

Her cheeks heated at the memory and she looked away.

Maybe this was a bad idea. Except she needed his help.

Regardless of whether or not he had any surveyor experience, as a rancher, he had to know more than her. That was the only reason she'd asked him to join her.

Not because her pulse spiked whenever his eyes landed on hers or he offered that boyish smile that always set her at ease. He had a way of doing that. Always had. He could sense tension, tell something was wrong, no matter how hard she tried to hide it. He'd try to distract her by acting goofy or cracking a joke. But every once in a while, like on that hot muggy Thursday afternoon so long ago, he simply listened.

And made her feel like she was the most important person in the world to him.

She paused and gazed toward the trees. "Funny, isn't it, how you and I both ended up back here?"

He swallowed and studied her as if wanting to say something, but then he just nodded.

"Remember those treats your mom used to always pack for us?" She sidestepped a large, prickly weed. "She was so sweet to me, treating me like I was the daughter she never had."

"Think she worried you needed a mother's touch, someone to talk to."

"Guess I did." She'd filled a hole Rheanna's uninterested, man-chasing mom had created. "I miss her." *And us.* "Is she still keeping herself busy sewing blankets for NICU babies and pregnant single moms?"

"When she has time. She stays pretty busy nowadays. She and my pop bought a grocery store about thirty minutes north of here."

"I remember." Apparently, they'd decided they'd had enough of ranching. She could certainly understand that. Raising horses was a hard, unpredictable way to make a living. A drought, fire—or in Dave's case, flood—could knock a ranch out, and just when they'd started to get their feet back under them, nature could wreak havoc once again.

She and Dave reached the edge of the last pasture and were venturing into uncut land. A warm breeze stirred the knee-length grass around them and the leaves and branches before them, creating a soft rustling sound that reminded her of God and His quiet whispers to a woman's heart.

She could sure use those whispers now—His guidance and assurance that she'd done the right thing in moving here. That she and Amelia would be okay.

Twigs snapped under their boots as they entered the shade of the forest. According to the map, and assuming the vegetation hadn't changed much, her property extended about three-quarters in. Though she could probably pay the Wiggenhorns a monthly fee to share the land that lay between her property and their hayfield. They weren't using that section anyway.

The wind swept a lock of hair across her face. She brushed it aside. "I'd love to hear more about your journey into ranching."

"After I graduated, I worked for my folks in their store for a while, but it wasn't for me. I felt cooped up. So, I started looking for ranch hand jobs."

"You always did like the outdoors."

He nodded. "I'd been working at a local ranch for going on two years, maybe three. I liked my boss, and he paid me well enough, but it was a dead-end job. His ranch had been in his family going on four generations, and he had two teen boys itching to step in and a great trainer nowhere near retirement. Watching him and those teens stirred something in me, made me want more."

A place of his own or a family? She'd never heard him

talk about kids. What if he didn't want to be a father? Then there couldn't be anything between them.

He swatted at a bug. "Like I mentioned, I was already in Wyoming, working for another rancher, padding my savings account as best as I could. When I saw the lease-to-own ad, I thought it was a scam but figured there was no harm in checking it out. So, I called the guy and we had a long chat. Turned out he was getting too old to manage the land and didn't have kids to follow in his footsteps. I suspect he worried some developer would come bulldoze it all and cover it in concrete. A couple years in, he needed to liquidate. I gave him some money down and he transferred the title and payments to me."

"And now? I saw an article on the flood. The rancher they interviewed said it was over for him and his family. That they'd been barely making ends meet before and didn't think they'd recover. What about you?"

"I've been knocked down before. The Bible says God will turn all things to good. Figure now's His chance to shine." He gave a half-hearted laugh.

She'd always admired his grit, and all he'd overcome. She couldn't imagine what he felt, seeing his ranch destroyed by all that flooding. And yet, he'd bounce back. She had no doubt.

But his every step forward would only lead him further from her.

They had a deep history together, had meant a lot to one another during a difficult time for each of them. And they'd moved on. She couldn't let the emotion of standing here, with him, so close to that tree he'd once carved their initials into, hinder her good sense.

Later that week, Dave stopped at Asha's stall to gauge her condition. Though he didn't see much in terms of weight gain, she appeared stronger and more alert. "Hey, girl. You want a treat?" He held out a peppermint, and she hesitantly approached. Her velvety hairs nuzzled his palm as she lipped up the candy. "You ready for some sunshine?" He'd already introduced her to the two other horses currently out to pasture, and they seemed to get along fine. "Bet you're anxious for your little one to come, huh?"

As was he, and not just due to his worry regarding the health of the foal. The mama wouldn't be able to gain weight eating for two. He ran a hand along her withers. Though she tensed, she didn't pull away. "That's a girl." He gently, slowly, put a halter on her, speaking kindly as he did. "You're safe here."

He'd just released her and was relatching the gate when Amelia ran up to him carrying an armload of buttercups, brown-eyed Susans and dandelions. "Would you like to buy some flowers?"

He chuckled. "Flowers, huh? You trying to earn money for something special?"

She nodded. "To buy Mommy a birthday gift. I'm making her a book, too, with pictures of me and her that will make her cry. But not on account of being sad. Happy tears."

A lump lodged in his throat as he remembered the first Mother's Day he wanted to buy anyone anything. He'd been living with his folks for maybe six months at the time and had just learned they were working toward adoption. But that wasn't what had touched him most. His mom had won his heart the month prior when she'd taken him for a late-night picnic, just the two of them.

What made their getaway extra special was the fact that he'd blown up, calling her all sorts of names, the day prior. She hadn't deserved a lick of that, nor had he been mad at her. But somehow, she always took the brunt of his emotions. His therapist had said that was because he was growing attached and was afraid she'd leave like everyone else in his life had. That he'd acted out to push her away before she could reject him.

But she'd done the opposite. When he'd given her every reason to kick him out, she'd held tight to him instead. That Mother's Day, he wanted to give her something to show just how much she meant to him. Only he didn't have any money, so, like Amelia, he'd tried to earn it any way he could.

He pulled his wallet from his back pocket, knowing he had maybe two tens in cash. He could always pop by the bank, not that he had a storehouse there, either. But when this sweet child peered up at him with her big, brown, hope-filled eyes, knowing he hadn't money to spare and operating on that truth were two different things.

"How much can I get for twenty bucks?"

"Um… They're ten cents each." She dropped the flowers on the ground and began to count them out, lost track at twelve, and started again.

He squatted to eye level, elbows propped on his knees. "You know what you want to buy your mama?"

She grinned and nodded. "Some really soft slippers, the pretty ones, pink or maybe purple, and a fuzzy blanket. She likes soft things, and to read books. Least, she used to, but she's too busy now." Her brow furrowed. "Or maybe I should get her a diary, for when she reads her Bible and talks to God."

"I'm sure she'd love those things, and I bet you could buy them for twenty bucks, which, looking at your flowers all laid out like they are, seems a fair trade to me."

"Yay!" She sprang to her feet and wrapped her arms around him.

He stiffened, then relaxed and returned her hug, his heart so full it seemed ready to explode. Though he'd never considered himself father material, moments like this could easily turn a fella into a family man.

Someday, maybe. When his finances were back in order, his ranch was running well and he found a lady with the grit to stick around through all of life's floods and windstorms.

He still hadn't made a decision about going into business with his buddy. It wasn't right to keep his friend hanging much longer. What was holding him back? Was he set on ranching alone or not ready to leave here?

He pulled away, and Amelia took a step back and brushed hair from her face with her forearms. "Could you take me to the store? To buy Mommy's presents and help me with her party? She never gets a party or gifts or anything, not even a card or nothing from my grandma. That's her mommy."

He raised his eyebrows. "A party?"

"Uh-huh. With balloons and a cake and those noisy things you blow? And decorations, too. And pretty napkins with unicorns or hearts or princesses on them. Mommy always calls me a princess, but I think she's just as pretty. Don't you, Mister Dave?"

He about choked. "What?"

"Do you think my mommy's pretty?"

His face heated. He averted his gaze and stood. Rheanna was the most beautiful woman, inside and out, he'd met, but he had no intention of stating that now. "When were you thinking of throwing this little shindig?"

Again, the girl's eyebrows pinched together. "On Sunday? With pretty food, like you see in restaurants—only we can't go to Wilma's on account I don't have enough money. Unless you want to buy more flowers. I could pick some more. Did you want me to? Would you buy them, Mister Dave, if I picked more flowers for you?"

He laughed, looking at the bundle he now owned. "How about I cook something up?"

"Yay! Like fried chicken or maybe pancakes or waffles with chocolate chips? No, lasagna. Mommy likes lasagna with lots of cheese, the white kind."

He'd been cooking for himself for over a decade, but nothing quite so involved. And yet, with it being for Rheanna, and knowing it was her birthday, he wanted to try. Plus, there was no way he could tell this sweet little peanut no, not when she looked up at him like that—like he was the solution to her every concern. "No problem. I'll handle supper, and I'll ask your mom if I can take you into town for a spell."

"Only don't tell her why." Amelia raised a finger, all serious-like. "It's a surprise."

"Right." Suppressing a laugh, he returned an equally serious expression. "I'll figure something out." They should probably have the party at his place, so they could set it all up without Rheanna knowing. That meant he'd need to find some way to get her over.

Amelia gave him another hug, then dashed off, her long brown hair swaying across her back.

Smiling, Dave returned to the stables, envisioning the look on Rheanna's face when she walked onto his back porch to see the party getup and her cake front and center, the flickering candles reflected in her eyes.

He was in deep.

This was a bad idea. But he couldn't back out now. He'd given Amelia his word, which meant he just needed to find a way to keep his emotions in check, something he'd clearly been failing to do.

Chapter Eight

Rheanna grabbed the pitcher of homemade crab apple cider and refilled the glasses around the table. "I can't thank you ladies enough for your help." The women gathered in her dining room, most of them from Lucy Carr's quilting club, had been such an encouragement to her. And now, hearing their enthusiasm for her trail ride idea made her feel like she could actually save the ranch and the rescue horses. They'd lifted her up so much that she'd felt confident about setting a date for the trail ride, and they'd all agreed to work toward that goal as fast as possible, since it wasn't that far off.

Lucy frowned. "Not trying to sound snarky or anything, but about those 'horse rentals' you talked about. You really sure that's necessary? Seems to me folks would expect this to be a B.Y.O.H. event. Bring your own horse."

Rheanna flipped through her packet of papers. "According to my research, these events can draw people interested in the experience, who maybe have only been riding a handful of times." Hopefully those were also the type of attendees who would be most likely to sign up on such short notice.

"Those folks aren't likely to be repeat customers." Janice, a woman with long black hair and deep smile lines, tapped the end of her pencil against her palm.

Rheanna nodded. "I figured as long as we're putting in all this work, we might as well open it up to whomever wants to come." Not to mention, they didn't have much time for a sophisticated promotional campaign. "I'd love to fill up our boarding stalls and lesson schedule, for sure. But I'm also hoping for donations. Dave's friend assured me we can receive tax-deductible funds while we wait for our nonprofit status to go through."

"Makes sense to me." Lucy gave a quick, firm nod. "Now that we know the what, let's figure out the how." Her wide grin triggered equally joyful expressions in everyone else. Then, turning more serious, she plunked her forearm on the table next to her tablet and raised a pen. "What all will we need?"

"Well, considering we haven't done trail riding in who knows how long, I should probably get the horses ready." Rheanna wrote herself a note. "See if Dave can train them a bit, then maybe have the Dillard boys take them on some practice runs."

She glanced at the time on her phone. Where was Ivy? She'd promised to join them for this meeting. Her absence stung.

"We need to connect to other nearby properties somehow," Janice said. "To lengthen the route."

Rheanna frowned. "That sounds complicated. I'm going to be lucky to get mine cleaned up in time."

"Don't you worry, dear." Lucy patted her hand. "Most folks been galloping across their land for generations now. You know, you should call the Owenses. They've got a historic bed-and-breakfast along with trail rides of their own about ten miles out of town. Pretty sure they'd welcome the exposure, maybe even enough to motivate them to help with prep."

Janice fluffed her hair. "They sold most of their land to Neil Landers. But he kept the trails and added to them. They go for quite a ways, actually. Bought up the property behind and beside him."

"Perfect." Lucy wrote on her page. "I'll call him this evening." She made eye contact with Rheanna. "The hill country's got riding trails all over the place."

The other women voiced agreement. "Think the Men of God would take care of food? Trinity Faith has one of those tailgate grills those fellas use for all their events."

Rheanna wrinkled her brow. "Men of God?"

"That's what the guys at church call themselves." Lucy jotted down more notes. "I think you should contact Wilma's. She'd welcome the exposure, I'm sure, and would cut us a deal. Then we could upcharge by 20 percent."

The women continued offering suggestions, ideas and people to call so fast Rheanna struggled to keep up. Their excitement lowered her anxiety another notch.

She smiled and returned to her seat. "Everyone should have such support." Her eyes stung with the threat of tears as she surveyed the precious band of women, the stitching-prayer-warriors as they liked to call themselves, all around her. "I can't tell you how much this means."

Lucy locked eyes with her. "Didn't I tell you, that first day I came over, that we gals wouldn't leave you to run this place alone?" She swept her arm wide to indicate the ranch. "I could tell by the glint in your eyes—a mixture of terror and doubt, neither of which I blame you for—that you didn't believe me. But I knew just as the drought follows the thunderstorm, I'd have opportunity to prove my words soon enough."

Rheanna gave her a sideways hug. "You have. All of

you, a hundred times over." She wasn't used to being on the receiving end of such goodwill and wasn't quite sure how to handle it. "I just wish there was some way I could give back, for all you ladies have done for me."

"Pshaw." Lucy flicked a hand. "It's not a blessing if it comes with strings attached."

The front door flew open, and Amelia blew in, dandelion fluff and straw in her windblown hair. The screen door slapped closed behind her.

"Mama! Mama! Can I go in town with Mister Dave? Please? He said he'd take me and that I wouldn't bother him none. I promise I wouldn't."

All heads turned her way, and Rheanna stood. Before she could respond, Dave walked in wearing his cowboy hat, boots and a snug, charcoal gray T-shirt that accentuated his muscular build.

"Ma'am." A smile lit his eyes when they met hers, and he held her gaze long enough for heat to climb into her face. Then he tipped his hat at the other women. "Ladies."

Rheanna excused herself from the table to meet him in the living room, where he stood with a bouncing and begging Amelia.

"Sorry." Rheanna offered a sheepish smile. "It appears she's taken a liking to you." He seemed to have that effect on people. Both she and Amelia were growing much too attached.

How much of Amelia's enthusiasm came from her longing for a father? Rheanna's heart sank at the thought.

"Nothing to apologize for. I like spending time with the little peanut." He winked at Amelia, causing her grin to widen, which in turn increased Rheanna's concern.

She loved that Dave was investing in Amelia, and he certainly seemed like a positive role model. But again she wondered what would happen once he left? Not only would his departure sadden her, but the vacancy could trigger wounds and insecurities related to her bio dad. She'd probably feel she'd been abandoned by two men, practically ensuring she developed daddy issues. How would that affect her future relationships—her ability to fall in love and maintain a healthy marriage?

Rheanna faced her daughter. "Sweetie, Mister Dave is busy."

Amelia crossed her arms with a groan and slumped. "You never let me go anywhere!"

"That's not true." Although she had to admit the nugget of truth underlying Amelia's statement. The poor girl did spend most of her time on the ranch, and often entertaining herself while Rheanna tried to keep the place running.

"I really don't mind her coming." Dave rested a hand on his belt buckle. "Unless you prefer she stayed home."

"Now isn't this the sweetest thing." Lucy came up beside Amelia and rested a hand on her shoulder. "And such a great example of the power of community. What's that people say—it takes a village? Well, we sure got that in Sage Creek, now don't we, dear?" She gave Rheanna's hand a squeeze. "Didn't we just pray this afternoon that God would help you get done everything that needed doing, for the ranch, the trail ride event, the rescue horses…"

Rheanna chewed the inside of her lip. She could use the extra time. "Sure. Let me grab her booster seat."

"I'll get it." He smiled.

"Thank you." If this little outing truly was an answer to prayer, then God would protect Amelia's heart, right?

Would He protect hers, as well?

He hadn't nearly twenty years ago when Dave walked out of her life in much the same way her father and her ex-

husband had—with nothing but a bunch of empty promises, shattering her world.

After her husband's betrayal, she'd determined never
to let anyone hurt her like that again. That was one promise she actually had control over, and she fully intended
to keep it.

Amelia chattered nonstop, hardly pausing to take a
breath as they drove into town. He would've expected to
find her boundless energy tiring, but the little princess had
the opposite effect. Her enthusiasm was an unexpected ray
of sunshine in the middle of a hard, stormy—literally and
figuratively—season. So much so that he found himself
wanting to prolong this jaunt as much as possible.

Stopped at a four-way, he shot Amelia a smile. "You
up for some hot cocoa and a pastry?" The rich aroma of
fresh brewed coffee and yeasty baked goods seeping into
his cab reminded him that he'd forgotten to eat lunch.

"Yeah!" Amelia beamed and bounced in her seat.

"The Sweet Spot it is." He parked in front of the bak-
ery/bookstore and cut the engine. "We might even find
something for your mama while we're here."

She hurried to unbuckle her seat belt and reached for
the door handle.

"Hold up, Princess." Granted, she was six and Sage
Creek folk tended to drive through town slowly with an
eye on pedestrians, but he didn't intend to take chances.
Especially considering the clear look of concern that had
flashed in Rheanna's eyes when he offered to take Amelia off her hands.

She didn't trust him, not like she used to. Although
part of him wanted to find some way to bridge the distance that time and hurt had wedged between them, there

Loyal Readers
FREE BOOKS Voucher

We're giving away

THOUSANDS of **FREE BOOKS**

LOVE INSPIRED
INSPIRATIONAL ROMANCE

To Protect
His Children

LINDA GOODNIGHT
NEW YORK TIMES BESTSELLING AUTHOR

He'll do anything to make sure they're cared for...

LARGER PRINT

Romance

LOVE INSPIRED SUSPENSE
INSPIRATIONAL ROMANCE

Alaskan
Rescue

TERRI REED

K-9 UNIT

ALASKA K-9 UNIT

LARGE

Suspense

Don't Miss Out! Send for Your Free Books Today!

Get up to 4 FREE FABULOUS BOOKS You Love!

To thank you for being a loyal reader we'd like to send you up to 4 FREE BOOKS, absolutely free.

Just write "YES" on the Loyal Reader Voucher and we'll send you up to 4 Free Books and Free Mystery Gifts, altogether worth over $20, as a way of saying thank you for being a loyal reader.

Try **Love Inspired® Romance Larger-Print** books and fall in love with inspirational romances that take you on an uplifting journey of faith, forgiveness and hope.

Try **Love Inspired® Suspense Larger-Print** books where courage and optimism unite in stories of faith and love in the face of danger.

Or **TRY BOTH!**

We are so glad you love the books as much as we do and can't wait to send you great new books.

So don't miss out, return your Loyal Reader Voucher Today!

Pam Powers

LOYAL READER
FREE BOOKS VOUCHER

YES! I Love Reading, please send me up to 4 FREE BOOKS and Free Mystery Gifts from the series I select.

Just write in "YES" on the dotted line below then return this card today and we'll send your free books & gifts asap!

➡ YES ⬅

Which do you prefer?

☐ **Love Inspired®
Romance
Larger-Print**
122/322 IDL GRJD

☐ **Love Inspired®
Suspense
Larger-Print**
107/307 IDL GRJD

☐ **BOTH**
122/322 & 107/307
IDL GRJP

FIRST NAME

LAST NAME

ADDRESS

APT.#

CITY

STATE/PROV.

ZIP/POSTAL CODE

EMAIL ☐ Please check this box if you would like to receive newsletters and promotional emails from Harlequin Enterprises ULC and its affiliates. You can unsubscribe anytime.

LI/SLI-520-LR21

wasn't much point. Her life was here, in Sage Creek, on the ranch he'd bolted the door to long ago.

Besides, she had a kid, and he hadn't a clue how to be a father. Growing up, he'd experienced enough bouncing from one foster home to another to learn there was a big difference between taking a little one out shopping and raising them day in and day out.

How much came naturally and how much could be learned—and unlearned?

Less than ten minutes later, with cocoa in hand, Amelia had temporarily forgotten about her mother's birthday and darted to the children's area. Figuring they weren't in any rush, Dave used the time to sift through a newspaper left on a nearby table. A classified ad reminded him to call his parents.

He found an empty table near the window in eyeshot of Amelia and tapped his mom's number.

"Dave." She sounded out of breath when she answered, like she'd run for the phone. "Dad and I were just talking about you. He heard of another great lead, at a Thoroughbred ranch in Kentucky. Some of their stallions have stud fees upward of five thousand dollars."

"Which means they've probably got world-class trainers, too."

"Don't sell yourself short, son. You're as fine a horseman as they come. Practically raised on a saddle."

He chuckled. "Thanks, Mom. I really appreciate you and Dad thinking of me. But I may have found something else." He told her about his friend's business offer.

"Interesting. You going to do it?"

His thoughts immediately jumped to Rheanna, her sweet smile, her chocolate-colored eyes that always held such an inquisitive look and her long brown hair.

He shook off the visual. "I've got a lot to think about."

He couldn't delay his decision much longer, and not just for his friend's sake. He'd managed to stay on top of his bills so far, but his savings were dipping low.

"Want to talk pros and cons?"

"Like old times, huh?" He laughed. "I appreciate it, but I'll figure this out."

What were his options? His friend's plans seemed solid. If he partnered with him, then maybe he could save his property. Otherwise, he might have to declare bankruptcy. That would practically ensure no bank would ever lend to him again, a huge problem, considering he'd need to repair his outbuildings and replace all his equipment. Both options would mean no more Rheanna or Amelia.

While staying in Sage Creek for any length of time could leave him nothing to rebuild on.

He feared it would also break his parents' hearts.

It seemed every option came at a cost.

Something clanked across the line. His mom released a loud breath. "Oh, boy. I better go see what kind of mess your dad got himself into this time."

He smiled. "No problem. Love you." He ended the call and watched Amelia sitting cross-legged on the floor, books spread all about her. That child sure could draw a fella in.

If he could figure out a way to hold out until next spring, when he'd be able to reseed all his grazing pastures—and on rich and fertile postflood soil...

He mentally calculated all the money he expected to come in—cash value for his insured equipment, minus his deductible. How aggressively was his buddy going after breeding Dave's mares and stallions? Regardless, Dave felt comfortable assuming he'd be able to bring in at least a quarter of what Dave had the year before. Especially considering the guy had a larger ranch with a reputation built through generations. Hopefully at least half of Dave's broodmares would foal...

He hadn't even considered training costs. His ranch had always been small enough that he'd handled that part on his own, but his friend's operation was too big for that. He stood and gazed toward the back of the store.

Amelia had gathered a couple stuffed animals off nearby shelves and was "reading" them a story. Her animation made him chuckle. That child was something else. Taking advantage of her make-believe time, he called Mitch to make training arrangements for any foals born come spring. And maybe get a better feel for his business proposition.

His buddy answered on the first ring. "My man. You're calling with good news I hope."

"Not sure about that yet, though I'm open to hearing more. How's the situation out there? My land still soggy?"

"Water's receding bit by bit. But yeah, your property's been slow."

"What about my broodmares?"

"Bred them all. We should know the success of our efforts soon enough."

"That's good. I appreciate all you're doing."

"Just trying to bootlick you into joining me, bud."

He laughed. "About that business venture. What kind of split were you thinking?"

"I don't want to be a hard nose or anything, considering our history. And I know your land will dry out, but..."

"You'll still have a lot more equity built in. I get that."

"However, you are one of the best trainers around. There's value in that. Honestly, I'd love to get a lawyer to help us, but I was thinking something like a 35 to 65 percent split."

"What's that mean as far as salary?"

"Let me crunch some numbers and shoot something your way. If you don't like what I come up with, counter."

Amelia headed toward him with both arms loaded with potential purchases, certainly much more than she had the funds to buy.

"Listen, I need to let you go. I'll be looking for your offer." Dave ended his call and tucked his phone into his back pocket. "What do you have there?"

She deposited her load onto the table, sending items spilling onto the floor. "I can't choose."

He picked up a cookbook with a picture of an iced bundt cake on the cover. "Your mama likes to bake?" He found this surprising, considering how often she burned things, a habit she'd had for as long as he'd known her. Although his mom had tried to teach her to cook and bake more than once, Rheanna always showed more interest in eating. He could relate.

"No, silly, that's for us."

"What?"

"So we can make her a cake."

"How about we buy her one?"

Amelia frowned. "But I don't have enough money."

"Tell you what. I'll pay for the cake and you can make the decorations." He ruffled her hair. "Deal?"

She grinned and wrapped her arms around him in a tight hug—an action he could get used to. "Deal."

"You choose a book and one other item for your mama, we'll let Ms. Leslie ring them up, then head to the store to see about getting your mom a cake."

They had just concluded their purchase, which included a sparkly gift bag and tissue paper, and were about to leave when Sally Jo breezed in.

She wore jean shorts, pink boots and a blinged-out cowgirl hat. "Dave, what a pleasant surprise." Her gaze landed on Amelia, and her smile twitched. "Babysitting duty?"

"Just running some errands with my little ranch-buddy."

"We're going to surprise my mama for her birthday, aren't we, Mister Dave? Only don't tell her. Promise?"

Sally Jo's expression tightened. "Oh, really? Sounds to me like your boss is making you her nanny and errand boy."

Dave tensed. "We best get going." With a tip of his hat and a hand to the back of Amelia's head, he led her out before Sally Jo could say anything else.

Unfortunately, the store was out of cakes and, since their baker only worked part-time, didn't anticipate having any until the following week.

The clerk shrugged. "Sorry. Most people order ahead."

Amelia's shoulders slumped. "But Mom's birthday is tomorrow."

"We've got mix—chocolate, lemon, spice, you name it—in aisle eight." The clerk pointed. "Just add all the ingredients and follow the instructions on the back."

"Uh…" Living as a bachelor, he'd learned to grill steaks, make spaghetti and cheesy potatoes, but he'd never tried baking.

"Yeah!" Amelia hopped up and down. "I love baking, only Aunt Ivy never wants me in the kitchen." She grabbed Dave's hand and tugged him toward aisle eight. "We'll need frosting, too. And candles and sprinkles and candy roses." She spoke so fast, Dave was practically breathless just listening.

Next, she tried to talk him into buying ingredients to make lasagna. Thankfully she agreed to the frozen variety, and soon they were heading back to the ranch.

The first place, once his parents adopted him, that

he'd considered home. After Rheanna's uncle stole that from him, he'd thought he'd closed his heart on the place for good. And now? His heart was shifting fast, and that scared him. Made him want to run or close off his emotions. But he couldn't let his fear or the pain of his past overshadow everything good.

He'd lived here, in Sage Creek, from age thirteen to midway through his sophomore year. This was where he'd first decided he wanted to be a rancher, just like his dad. Not his bio dad. He'd never known him, but the man who stood beside him, who spoke hope into his life. One summer working alongside his dad and hearing, "Good job, son," was all it took. The feel of the sun on his face and the way the air whizzed by when he galloped across the open field, just him and his horse...

That was the freest he'd ever felt.

"Are you sad?"

He glanced at Amelia to find her watching him with a furrowed brow. "No, princess. I'm happy, because I'm with my little buddy."

She smiled. "Me?"

"Yep."

"I'm happy, too."

Her words stirred the ache for family that had followed him from home to home as a kid, only this time, he longed for fatherhood.

But what did he know about parenting? Prior to his adoption, his role models hadn't been all that great. What if he turned out to be a terrible dad? That wouldn't be fair to Amelia or Rheanna.

He turned onto the two-lane highway leading out of town. "How're we going to do all this without spoiling the surprise?"

"Can we make the cake at your house?"

"Won't your mom wonder where you are?"

"She's got Bible study tonight, with Ms. Lucy. And Ivy will be busy making her vitamin bars."

He laughed at how she wrinkled her nose at that last statement. "All right, then. Come on over after dinner and we'll get to baking."

About three hours later, she arrived at his cabin with a bucket filled to near overflowing with craft supplies.

He raised an eyebrow. "What's all this?"

"Stuff to make party decorations. Will you help me?"

Oh, boy. This was turning out to be much more complicated than he'd anticipated. "I'm really not the creative type."

"You mean you don't know how?"

"You could say that."

"I'll teach you." She looked up at him with such hope, such joy, he couldn't possibly decline.

"Let's get going on the cake first."

Amelia did most of the mixing and stirring, splattering egg goo and shell bits onto his counter.

He poured the batter in a greased pan and placed it in a preheated oven. "You want to lick the bowl?"

She nodded and soon her face was covered in chocolate. Laughing, he handed her a rag as they moved to the table, where she'd spread out her art supplies.

Halfway through coloring a sign he'd written block letters on, she paused and studied him. "Missy's daddy picked her up from Vacation Bible School today. To take her on their daddy-daughter date. That's what he called it. A daddy-daughter date. What do you think they did?"

"Oh, I don't know. Maybe got hot cocoa or something."

"Like we did?"

His heart squeezed. "Yeah, just like that."

She picked up her crayon, started to color, then stopped. "Is this what daddies do, too?"

Her question shocked the words from him. "I…uh… What do you mean?"

"Make cakes and presents for mommies and stuff?"

He swallowed. "I don't know." Truth was, he didn't, not really.

She angled her head. "Didn't you have a daddy?"

"Not for a long time, no."

"Did that make you sad?"

"Sometimes." A memory from his fourth grade year resurfaced. It'd been "take your child to work" day. Nearly his entire class had participated, leaving but a handful of them to suffer through some lame movie on various careers. Staring at a room filled with so many empty desks, he'd never felt quite so alone. So different.

His prayers for a family had intensified after that, then died after his eighth or ninth placement. By the time he'd met his adoptive parents, he'd given up hope that things could ever be different.

Praise God for unexpected surprises and the welcoming arms that, finally, after a lifetime of living as an outsider with no permanent place to land, made him feel like he belonged.

"Did all your friends have daddies?" Her voice was soft.

A lump lodged in his throat. He nodded.

"Mine, too. That makes me sad. Mama, too. Only she pretends it doesn't." She picked up a glitter stick. "She doesn't like anyone to see her cry, not even me."

He remembered that about her, the overly cheerful exterior she'd often presented. But as they began to spend time together, talking about stupid stuff at first, then dreams for their future, she started to open up. To let him comfort her.

So much had changed.

His heart wrenched, for Amelia and Rheanna, and for what once had been—what could've been.

Chapter Nine

❧

Rheanna sat on the couch, working through the mound of paperwork shoved in the shoeboxes at her feet. "How did my uncle manage to avoid getting audited until now? These records are a mess."

"You said he had Alzheimer's, right?" Ivy dropped another container of documents, which she'd found in a storage area beneath the stairs, on the floor.

"Early onset, yeah. I don't know for how long."

"It probably came on gradually, without Bill noticing or even thinking to step in until things got out of hand. Any chance the IRS will take that into consideration?"

"That might earn some sympathy, but if we can't verify our claims, they'll still want their money." Money she didn't have. They were barely scraping by as it was.

"How are we doing on getting new boarders in?"

Rheanna sighed. "Even with the horse rescues, we've still got empty stalls. I get the feeling people are concerned with our knowledge of proper horse care." Not that she blamed them, especially with the high staff turnover they'd experienced. "Most folks view us as a couple of city girls riding on my inheritance."

"But we've got Bill and Dave."

She shrugged and resumed sorting through invoices.

T-Bone barked at something outside, most likely a squirrel or rabbit.

Ivy pulled her phone from her back pocket and glanced at the screen. "You know what you need? A night out with your bestie." She took the paper Rheanna had been holding and set it on the coffee table. "How about I call Lucy and see if she'll come babysit?"

"I'm not in the mood."

"So, get in the mood. It's your birthday, for goodness sakes."

That was, in part, precisely why she didn't want to go. Birthdays had always caused more pain than joy. Growing up, they'd felt like an afterthought, if not forgotten entirely. Yet one more proof of just how unimportant she'd been to her mother.

"Come on." Ivy grabbed Rheanna's hands and attempted to tug her to her feet. "It's bottomless fries night at Wilma's."

"Like you'd let a deep-fried carb pass through that heavily guarded mouth of yours."

"For my bestie on her birthday, absolutely." She grinned. "What do you say?"

"I'd say, I'm broke."

"This one's on me, girlfriend."

Rheanna would rather Ivy contribute to groceries or the utility bill. "I appreciate the thought, but honestly, I'm content to spend my evening right here, curled up with a book and a hot cup of peppermint tea."

"Fine. If you want to mope around here, buried in bills and paperwork, that's on you. But I'm going stir-crazy." Hands on her hips, she stared at Rheanna for a moment, as if hoping she'd change her mind. Then, with a huff, she marched off toward her room.

Rheanna spent the next couple of hours going through her uncle's old financials, half of which she didn't understand. She tried calling Bill, but he didn't answer, so she left him a voice mail. "I'd really like your help with this IRS stuff. Can you set aside a few hours this week to walk me through it?"

It frustrated her that he seemed so uninterested in resolving this. She understood he was busy. Granted, she was partially to blame for that, as they were still understaffed. But he had to know, if the IRS came after her and she lost the ranch, he'd be out of a job.

Then again, he could probably find employment on another ranch easy enough. But her? She'd have to completely uproot Amelia, again, not to mention Ivy. Where would she work? She could maybe return to Grand Rapids and beg her former boss to take her back. He might even do it, but he'd probably make her work nights and weekends again. That would leave her zero time with Amelia.

The front door banged open. "Mama!" Amelia breezed in, her cheeks rosy and her forehead and nose glistening. "I need to show you something."

Rheanna stood, her stomach tightening. "Is everything okay? Is it the horses?" She'd been keeping a close eye on Asha, fully aware the poor girl could go into labor any day but hoping she'd hold out to full term.

Amelia shook her head so fast, her hair swooshed in front of her face. "It's a surprise. Come on."

Rheanna smiled. Her sweet little princess, always such a thoughtful one. She'd been systematically redeeming birthdays—and all other celebrations, about half of which Amelia created—one handmade gift at a time.

"I love surprises." Rheanna let Amelia pull her out of the house and down the porch steps. "Where are you taking me?"

Amelia paused and faced her mother. "Close your eyes."

Oh, boy. That was an accident waiting to happen. "I don't think that's such—"

"Come on. Please." Her voice and expression were filled with such anticipation, such joy, how could Rheanna decline?

"All right. But walk slow."

Amelia nodded, waiting for Rheanna to comply, then led her farther from the house. "No peeking."

"Nope."

She paused again. "Hold on." She dashed off toward the house and returned with one of Ivy's fancy scarves. "Put this on, and tie it real tight, so you can't see anything."

Rheanna laughed. "You don't trust your mother, huh? I see how it is." She took the silky fabric, wrapped it around her eyes and head and secured it. Once again, she allowed her daughter to lead her forward—when what she wanted to do was snatch her sweet, tenderhearted girl in a hug. To treasure every childlike moment.

The ground beneath her changed from gravel to grass, then back to gravel again. They were heading north, and based on the scent of sunbaked hay, had just passed the boarding stables. "Where are we going?"

"You'll see."

They continued on to what felt like an uneven dirt road, similar to the one leading to the ranch hand cabins. Beyond them lay an expanse of trees—one of Amelia's "secret" forts, perhaps? "You're not going to lead us into spiderwebs or a poison oak patch, are you?"

"Mama, don't be silly." Amelia nudged her left. "Do you like Mister Dave?"

The question nearly made her stumble. "What?"

"Mister Dave. Do you like him?"

"He's nice." And kind and strong and gentle and thoughtful. Great with Amelia. Like he really cared for her. Everything a woman could want in a man. But his heart, his life, was elsewhere. In Wyoming.

"Do you think he's funny and handsome?"

Her face burned. "He's been a great help to the ranch, and he does a wonderful job with the horses."

"But he could be your boyfriend, right? And take you to the movies and to dinner and tell you you're beautiful?"

She stopped walking. "Has Aunt Ivy been letting you watch her chick flick movies with her again?"

Amelia's sigh was audible. "But, Mama, you like him, don't you? Because he likes me. He likes to be with me and teach me things and stuff. He said I'm funny and keep him young. Plus, he's going to let me help with the baby horse, once he's born. Or she. Do you think it'll be a he foal or a she foal?"

Rheanna wanted to take her blindfold off to see Amelia's face, to see if this conversation was stirring as many emotions within her as it was within Rheanna. "I don't know, sweetie."

"The baby won't have a daddy. Can you get her one?"

Tears pricked Rheanna's eyes. "I don't think so, sweetie." Amelia's words reminded her of all the child had lost when her father had walked out. A strong, positive male influence to lean on and look up to—not that Rheanna's ex had ever been all that positive. If only she'd paid more attention to the warning pings in her heart, but then she never would've had Amelia, her little princess and frequent shadow.

They turned left, and the gravel beneath them gave way to patches of grass and twigs.

After a few more steps, Amelia stopped her and gently

rotated her ninety degrees. "When I say, you can look. Ready? One, two, three. Look!"

Grinning so wide, it felt as if her cheeks were stretched, Rheanna slowly untied the scarf. She sucked in a breath. What was— Dave stood on his back porch, to the left of his patio table, covered in a pink, unicorn tablecloth and three place settings.

"Happy birthday, Mama!" Giggling, Amelia bounded up the porch steps, which were decorated with pink and purple streamers. A banner made from crayon-colored construction paper hung above and behind Dave, who stood there, looking shy and awkward, reminding her of the teen she'd once loved. The guy who could be bold as a stallion one minute, bumbling like a timid middle schooler the next.

Tucking her hair behind her ear, she straightened and slowly ascended the steps. "What's this about?"

"It's your birthday, duh!" Amelia rolled her eyes so dramatically, Rheanna couldn't help but laugh.

"I see that. But…" She met Dave's gaze, thinking back to a birthday, so many summers ago, that had meant the world to her. That day, Dave had given her the gift that had left her giddy for months after. He'd asked her to be his girl.

Dave Brewster, the kid who had turned the heads of practically every girl in Sage Creek, had chosen her.

For a time.

"Mister Dave, can we give her the present now?" Amelia bounced on the balls of her feet, her eyes bright.

Dave laughed. "How about we eat first, so the lasagna doesn't get cold." He pulled out a chair for Rheanna and motioned for her to sit, then ambled into his cabin with a chattering Amelia following close behind.

The tenderness in Dave's eyes whenever he looked at

Amelia, and the pure life and joy in hers, brought tears to Rheanna's. Stirred a hope within her she'd long tried to bury.

What would it be like to have a parenting partner? Someone to share the burden with, her anxieties with and to process all the well-intended advice the older ladies at Trinity Faith often provided? True, she had a community standing behind her, or at least, that's what Lucy assured her again and again. But every child needed a father.

She of all people understood that.

But she refused to chase after some man, especially one as transient as Dave, to fill that role. That would only hurt Amelia all the more. Rheanna had spent a lifetime playing seconds to her mother's constantly changing boyfriends, a pain she intended to keep her daughter from experiencing.

Even if it meant shutting her heart off to love?

She suppressed a sigh.

Dave emerged from his house again, this time carrying a steaming baking dish. "Munchkin here told me this was your favorite." He winked at Amelia. "An absolute must-have for the birthday girl."

Lasagna? Rheanna blinked, struggling to process it all. More accurately, not wanting to process it.

Her throat felt scratchy. "Thank you."

He smiled. "My pleasure. Now eat up, before it gets cold." He nudged Amelia, and she giggled, clearly overjoyed with how their surprise turned out.

And with good reason. This was by far the best birthday Rheanna could remember.

Halfway through their meal, Amelia wiped her mouth with the back of her hand, streaking her cheek with tomato sauce. "Can we sing the birthday song now?"

Dave chuckled and eyed her plate. "But you've hardly eaten your dinner."

"That would make me too full for cake."

"Can't beat that logic." He grinned and shot Rheanna a wink that turned her insides to mush. He stood, gathering plates, and made eye contact with Amelia. "Want to help me with the candles?"

"Yeah!" She sprang from her seat and the two of them hurried into the kitchen, leaving Rheanna to fight conflicting emotions. She so longed for more of this. The three of them, gathered around a dinner table, laughing and talking. To always see such joy on Amelia's face, and the adoration on Dave's whenever he addressed the child.

For more birthdays to come, not just hers, but Amelia's, as well. For lazy summer afternoons, sipping lemonade on the porch swing. For vacations and Christmases and all those family moments Rheanna had felt she herself missed.

What did Dave want? Sure, he was here now, serving cake and lasagna. But what about when life felt hard? Where would he be then?

The screen door opened, and he and Amelia emerged, her carrying the cake while he hovered nearby, as if ready to catch it. No doubt Amelia had picked the candle—a chunky pink unicorn with a purple wick.

"Happy birthday to you," they sang in unison, Amelia's full-on outside voice rising above Dave's smooth baritone.

"Your mama's a monkey," Amelia belted out with a giggle, nearly dropping the cake. Dave grabbed the plate beneath it and helped her set it smoothly on the table. "And you live in the zoo."

Rheanna laughed. "Is that right?"

They continued to banter, Amelia adding more made-up lyrics to the song, while Dave dished out slices, acting as if this evening was the highlight of his day.

As if this moment meant as much to him as it did to Rheanna.

Sitting here, on Dave's porch, seeing all this—the time, thought and energy—emotions she'd long since suppressed, dangerous emotions, surged to the surface.

She shouldn't be here. Clearly her heart was too fragile, her resolve too weak. But she couldn't leave now. Sweet little Amelia would be crushed. Rheanna would just have to woman up. Act like the mature adult, the ranch boss, that she was. And that was all she was to Dave—his boss. He was her employee—very temporary employee.

Come fall, if not by month's end, he'd be gone, back to his ranch in Wyoming. Once again leaving Rheanna far behind, only not with a broken heart. Not this time.

But could they be friends? Could they somehow salvage the connection they'd once had? And if that was the extent of their relationship, was she strong enough, emotionally, to remain just friends? Or would her heart always long for more?

Dave watched with amusement as Amelia asked one question after the other: Was her mom surprised? Did she think everyone had forgotten? She knew Amelia would never forget, didn't she? Would she have picked lasagna? Did she like it with the white cheese or the orange?

Rheanna was an amazing mother. Kind, gentle, attentive. She answered patiently, as if this moment here, with her daughter, was the highlight of her day.

How'd she feel about Dave sharing this evening with them? She'd visibly stiffened, when, after removing her scarf, her eyes had met his. A flash of sorrow followed. Why? Because she missed him, missed what they'd once had?

Or did his presence remind her of Amelia's father? Did

she wish he were standing here, celebrating her birthday, instead?

Thinking this way wouldn't do either of them any good. He cleared his throat. "I called Drake Owens, spoke with him and his pops."

Rheanna's expression brightened. "And?"

"They're all in. In fact, Drake's mom—don't remember her name—she's taking it upon herself to call the other farmers and ranchers and anyone with land to see if they'll accommodate. And Drake's working to drum up all the manpower possible to help get your trails rideable again, which shouldn't take much. Hack through a few roots, trim things back a bit."

Talking business plans made sharing a meal with Rheanna, sitting close enough to smell her soft floral perfume, feel safer. Less intimate.

Less like family.

Which they weren't. Though at one time he'd dreamed about moments just like this.

She rubbed her pinkie nail with her thumb. "Think maybe we can actually pull this off?"

"Figure we kind of have to." Once the temperatures dipped, Rheanna wouldn't be able to rely so heavily on grazing land. With the cost of hay skyrocketing like it was...

She set her glass down. "How long do you plan on staying?"

He swallowed, feeling sweet little Amelia's eyes on him. "Have you had any response from your help wanted ad?"

She dropped her gaze. "Not really."

"Send me what you wrote up and I'll get it posted to online boards." That was about all he could tell her. He knew he couldn't stay here forever.

He took a swig of water. "You set a date, and we're making it happen."

"I know." She took in a sharp breath. "I hope we can pull it off that soon?"

"Like I said, we kind of have to." And not just because of winter or for his future business prospect. The longer he stayed here, working with the woman he once loved, looking into her big brown eyes, the greater the risk of him leaving in the same mess he'd found himself in the last time.

Heart tied to a girl who had no interest in him.

Unless… What if things could be different this time?

Amelia downed the rest of her juice. "Do you like surprises, Mama?"

"From you, always." Her gaze shot to Dave, questions filling her eyes. Questions he worried, were she to ask, he wouldn't be able to answer. Not for her or himself.

Amelia glanced back toward the kitchen. "Can I make some more art?"

Rheanna smiled. "Of course."

"Yay!" She slid from her chair and darted back into the cabin, returned with her arms and hands full of paper, markers and crayons. "I'm going to make flash cards for the horses. So I can teach them to read. I think they'd like pretty ones, don't you, Mister Dave?"

"Created by you? Absolutely."

He thought again of the question Amelia had asked earlier. *Is this what daddies do?* If so, if this was what fatherhood looked like, he could sure get used to it.

Someday.

Amelia deposited her items on the table, sending crayons and markers rolling every which way. "Can Jasmine come over to help, Mama? She's my new friend from VBS. She's really nice."

"I'll ask her mother."

"Yay!" Amelia's wide grin triggered his, as well.

That girl sure had a way of bringing joy into every situation.

"Will you draw my hand, Mister Dave?" Amelia pressed her palm, fingers spread, onto a sheet of paper.

"Absolutely." He traced an outline using a purple marker.

"Now yours." She pointed to a clean portion of the page.

Once he was done, she asked her mom to do the same so that Amelia's handprint sat in the center of his and Rheanna's, though they'd had to squish their fingers together to make them fit, and even then, they'd run out of room.

"These are our kindness hands." Amelia wrote a *k* at the top of her page, then paused and looked at Dave. "How do I spell *kindness*? I forgot."

He smiled and spelled it out for her.

"We should teach the horses that word, too. Don't you think, Mr. Dave? That way they can all be friends and won't act mean to one another. We learned that in VBS. That God wants us to use our hands and our mouths to be nice to each other."

"Your teacher is a wise woman." He grabbed the yellow marker. "Mind if I join you?"

"Sure!" Amelia beamed, as if he'd just offered to take her to Six Flags.

Dave colored for a moment, enjoying the connection something as simple as a box of markers could create, then shifted to face Rheanna. "Any news on your end on connecting our trails to our neighbor's properties?" Whatever the Owenses drummed up would help but probably wouldn't be enough.

"I met with some ranchers this morning. Thankfully, most folks are willing to work with us."

"For a fee?"

She shook her head. "For free. Except for Mr. Hayes. He's demanding funds we simply don't have."

Dave exhaled. "Probably the most important chunk of land of all, as far as our event goes." The Hayes's property sat smack-dab in the center of their planned route.

"Yeah. Might be worth it to give him something. Not what he's asking, by any means, but whatever's fair for a day's use."

"I worry, if we do that, other ranchers might hear about it and get riled up."

Her face indicated she hadn't thought of that.

Lord, we're acting in faith here and trusting that You'll work everything out.

And if they couldn't pull this off? Rheanna could still lose the ranch.

Dave stacked the dirtied plates on top of each other and stood. "Don't worry. We'll figure all this out. And throw the best event Sage Creek's horse community has seen."

Amelia glanced up at him. "I can make posters for it! Like they have in the windows at VBS. Only with a lot more colors. And horses."

"Then we'll have a successful ride for sure." He bopped her on the nose, producing a giggle.

He'd make sure of it, because he had no intention of letting Rheanna or her daughter down.

Chapter Ten

Dave stopped outside Asha's stall to find the poor girl pacing and acting restless. Uncomfortable. Colic or signs of early labor? Either worried him. Either could kill her. Colic was one of the primary causes of death in healthy horses, which Asha was not. She was stronger than when they found her, but still had a long way to go.

She could also be experiencing pregnancy complications, many of which could be life-threatening to her and the foal. Dave had dealt with a few emergency births over the years, but never those involving a malnourished horse.

"How you doing, girl?" He moved toward the gate, but Asha stepped back, obviously trying to distance herself.

He shot Rheanna a text, asking her to pop in ASAP, then called the vet. Unfortunately, he got Wallow's voice mail. "Hey, Doc. I'm afraid we might have a situation on our hands." He relayed his observations. "We'd be mighty obliged if you headed this way and gave our girl a look-see."

He spent the rest of the afternoon working nearby, popping in regularly, in case the mare's situation turned critical. And checking the time on his phone nearly obsessively.

What if Asha was in crisis and the vet didn't arrive in time? Who else could he call?

He searched through his contacts for the names and numbers of the ranchers he'd talked with at the wedding. They'd seemed knowledgeable, although he wasn't certain their experience exceeded his. Still, wouldn't hurt to get an extra set of hands out here.

He started to call Cal then stopped. This wasn't technically an emergency. Yet. He'd give the vet a bit more time so as not to use up all his SOS's unnecessarily.

The soft footsteps characteristic of Rheanna approached from behind. He set his broom against the wall and turned to face her. "Hey. You got my message?"

She nodded, worry lines etched across her forehead. "I came as soon as I could. What's up?"

"I'm worried about our timid mama." He led the way to Asha's stall, explaining as they walked. "If Doc's right, she shouldn't be foaling for another couple of weeks. But honestly, I'm surprised her little one held on this long, that this pretty little lady conceived at all, considering everything she went through."

Malnourished, the stress of whatever abuse she experienced prior to rescue, not to mention the trauma she must've felt when transported here. But she'd been settling down some, growing more curious.

Rheanna rubbed at her collarbone like she often did when nervous or upset. "What now?"

"Hopefully Doc Wallow isn't off at some remote ranch tending to an emergency." He scrubbed a hand over his face. "Sure wish this sweet thing wasn't so skittish around me. Though most broodmares prefer to be left alone during the initial stages of labor, they usually tolerate a fella being nearby. On the ready, in case anything goes wrong."

"I imagine she'll hardly notice who or what's in her

stall, once her contractions get stronger." She cast the horse a worried glance. "And if it's colic?"

"Too bad we don't know much of her history—if she's been bred before, has ever had colic or dystocia. Guess we better prepare, just in case."

"How can I help?"

"Pray that this is the first stage of labor and that all goes smoothly?" He offered a slight smile. "And maybe keep trying to get a hold of the vet. In the meantime, I say we assume she's foaling. I'll add extra hay in her stall, about knee-high, so the baby has a soft place to land. Can you grab some gauze from the tack room so I can wrap her tail when it comes time—assuming she lets me near her."

"Sure." She hurried off and quickly returned with what he'd asked for.

They stayed there, shoulder to shoulder, watching the mare for about fifteen minutes longer, and for a moment, he imagined what life might be like, were his and Rheanna's lives to merge.

She had grit. She'd stayed calm under pressure and wasn't afraid of hard work. He'd always wanted a woman to work the ranch with. A woman who didn't mind getting dirty or breaking a nail, someone who loved horses as much as he did.

After his last relationship, he'd given up on finding that. But now?

Now, standing here, surrounded by the smell of horse and hay, with the woman he'd loved so deeply, now he wondered what might happen if he allowed himself to dream again.

Of true love that lasts and a family of his own.

After about twenty minutes, Rheanna said, "I should probably head to the house. Make sure Amelia gets dinner and her bath. I'll come back after I tuck her in."

"No need. I'll text you if anything changes."

"I want to."

The look in her eyes, so close to what he used to see when she peered up at him all those years ago, stalled his breath.

But then she averted her gaze and took half a step back, as if distancing herself from him. "Like I said, I'll be back."

And then she left, leaving him to process it all.

He'd come to Sage Creek apprehensive enough, not knowing who or what he'd encounter, expecting his reunion, however brief, with Rheanna to sting some. For a moment, soon forgotten once he returned home. Only there was no forgetting her. But he wasn't naive enough to believe they could just pick up where they'd left off, either. So much had changed. They'd created lives for themselves.

But what if God was offering them a second chance? What if that was part of why Dave was here?

Only his life was in Wyoming.

He released a breath and scrubbed a hand over his face. All his fretting and wondering would only give him a headache.

If not a heartache.

He needed to focus on Asha, on doing all he could to save both mare and baby.

As dusk settled over the ranch, the steady chirping of crickets punctuating the night air, Dave brought a folding chair, bottle of water and book into Asha's stall. Eyes on him, she took a step back, widening the distance between them.

"Don't worry about me." He set his chair in the northeast corner. "I'm just settling in. Think of me as a temporary stall mate." Why hadn't the vet returned his call?

Then again, he'd been coming out pro bono. Maybe they'd exhausted his generosity.

A fella had to pay his bills, after all.

As did Dave. Not to mention, he needed to make a trip out to his property to check on the damage. He couldn't honestly evaluate his friend's proposition before then.

That meant a fifteen-hour drive or plane ticket.

He set his phone on his lap, grabbed his book—a biography on Jim Gober, a nineteenth-century Texas cowboy and sheriff.

He'd just finished a chapter when Rheanna appeared, holding a thermos and freezer bag of rolls in one hand, crocheted blanket in the other. She'd pulled her long, wavy hair on top of her head in a messy bun, a few tendrils framing her face. Her auburn highlights shimmered a deeper shade in the dim barn lighting.

He stood to greet her with a tip of his hat, his thoughts momentarily stalled by her beauty. "Hey."

A slight blush colored her high cheekbones. "Hi. Hungry?"

"A bit. Thanks."

She opened the stall gate and stepped inside, her gaze bounced to the mare, halting, then returned to him.

"She'll be all right." He motioned to the chair.

She entered but remained standing, leaning back against the stall wall. "Considering how muggy it is out here, I'm not sure why I brought this." She lifted the blanket. "Habit, I guess."

He smiled. "I appreciate it." She'd developed quite a maternal side, one he found captivating.

She remained standing for a moment, one arm crossed over her chest, hand rubbing her tricep, then slid to the hay-covered ground.

Dave sat beside her, watching her from the corner of his

eye. Thinking back to a night, so long ago, when they'd sat shoulder to shoulder, just like this. She'd planned to go home that weekend for some one-on-one time with her mom, who'd promised to take Saturday off so they could go shopping, to dinner, the movies. But then, the day before she was supposed to pick Rheanna up, her mom canceled. Apparently, her latest boyfriend had something special planned.

Seeing her cry that night had torn him up inside. That was when he'd realized how much he loved her. In that moment, as he wrapped an arm around her and she leaned into his embrace, he'd promised himself he'd do whatever he could to protect her.

Less than a week later, she was mourning her beloved Bella. Because of him.

A few days after that, he and his family left.

"You think Asha will be okay?" Her voice was so quiet, he barely heard her.

"I hope so." Sitting next to Rheanna, inhaling the sweet scent of her floral perfume and fruity hair, he wanted to pull her close. To hold her like he used to.

But to what end? He didn't plan on staying. Couldn't.

She angled her head toward him. "Any updates on your ranch back home?"

He shrugged. "Place is still soggy, but most of the water has subsided." He picked up a piece of straw and snapped it between his fingers. "I put your ad for a full-time trainer on a bunch of equestrian boards. Figure you'll be getting calls anytime now."

Her brows pinched together, and she returned to studying the horse.

"I'll stick around to help whoever you hire get his feet under him, make sure he's a good fit." The moment the words were out of his mouth he regretted them. Not because he didn't want to help, but what if she couldn't find someone, or it took her months to do so?

No sense fretting about all these what-ifs. "How are things going with your IRS stuff?"

She sighed. "It's such a mess. It doesn't help that my uncle's writing is worse than chicken scratch, not to mention he seems to use some sort of shorthand or code. I can't understand half of the invoices I read. Nor have I found the documents the IRS requested."

The defeat in her voice stirred his protective side. "Maybe I can help." He at least understood ranching—the language, typical expenses and whatnot. "I have managed to get more students in—"

"Really? That's terrific!"

The lilt in her voice warmed him. "But I'm free tomorrow until about one. Other than stable chores. I can stop by the house, pick up wherever you've left off."

She leaned into him and hugged his arm, sending a jolt through him and making him reluctant to move for fear of breaking the moment.

"Thank you." She lifted her dark brown eyes, the color of espresso, to his. "Seriously. For everything you've done, are doing. I know this, being here in the first place, is a sacrifice. And I appreciate it."

His gaze dropped to her soft, pink mouth as memories of his lips on hers resurfaced, stirring feelings that would only complicate matters. Feelings that were becoming increasingly hard to deny or ignore.

Rheanna's phone rang, startling her. She glanced at the screen. "It's Wallow." She answered. "Hello, thanks for getting back to us." She relayed the situation and answered his questions.

"I'm on my way now. Should be there in ten minutes."

"Thanks."

Dave's stance conveyed quiet assurance, but she could see the apprehension in his eyes. "He's coming?"

She nodded and took a deep breath, thankful to know they'd soon have answers but fearing what they might be.

"It'll be okay." Dave wrapped an arm around her shoulder and gave a squeeze. "God didn't bring these creatures here to let them die. We've got to believe that."

She offered her best attempt at a smile. "I appreciate you."

His gaze locked on hers, and she got the sense that maybe he wanted to say something, or maybe to ask her something.

He lifted his hat, raked a hand through his hair and released a loud breath. "How about we pray for this little lady and her foal."

"I would love that."

He took her hand in both of his, sending a surge of warmth through her. "Lord, whatever's going on with this mare might be more than we can handle, from a human perspective. But we know nothing's too hard for You. You're the God of the impossible. Show us what to do, and help us turn this all—Asha, these horses, this ranch, my ranch…" His voice turned husky. "All that involves us and concerns us, over to You." He paused. "And bless that little princess Amelia and her mama." He gave her hand a squeeze. "In the name of your precious Son, amen."

That he'd prayed for her and Amelia brought tears to her eyes. She remembered a time when he'd seemed against religion, or at least, uninterested in it. He'd obviously changed, and for the better.

They had been kids, after all. Deeply hurting kids.

It struck her how much life he'd lived since she'd known him last. The edge of anger that she used to catch glimpses of every now and again seemed gone completely, replaced by a peace she found comforting.

The rhythmic thud of boots echoing in the aisle alerted her to Dr. Wallow's presence. She hurried out to meet him, Dave following close behind. "Thanks so much for coming on such short notice." And for free. She had to be near exhausting the man's generosity, though she suspected this was likely the first of many such emergency calls to come.

"Sorry I didn't get here sooner."

"We're just glad you're here." Dave greeted him with a handshake, then led the way to Asha's stall while Rheanna caught the vet up on all they'd observed.

Wallow watched the mare for a bit and scratched his jaw. "She's pretty worked up." He looked at Rheanna. "You okay with sedation?"

"Of course."

She waited, watching from the other side of the stall gate, while he performed his exam. Dave hovered inside the stall, looking like he had to constrain himself not to jump in and help. He clearly loved that horse. He'd taken to her immediately, always stopping by her stall, speaking kindly to her. Staying by her side, in that stiff chair.

Once finished, the vet pulled off his shoulder-length gloves and walked over to Rheanna. "She's suffering from uterine torsion."

"What does that mean?"

"Her uterus is twisted."

She winced. That sounded so painful. "Is that serious?"

The vet nodded. "Possibly life-threatening."

Her stomach sank. "Can you fix it?"

"Possibly, although it'll be expensive—with no guarantees. Financially, your best option is for me to get some folks out to help me rotate her manually, but I don't recommend that at this stage in her pregnancy. The risks are just too high—potential placenta detachment. Death of mom and baby."

She swallowed. "Our other option?"

"You can put her—"

"No." Dave's voice was low but firm.

The vet looked from him to Rheanna. She nodded her agreement.

"Your other option is surgery. But even then, mom and baby might not survive. Less than 60 percent of mares and foals do, and considering mama's health going in... But at least y'all caught her early. That'll help."

Her eyes stung with tears, and she stared at the hay at her feet. Dave came to her side and grabbed her hand, as if offering strength.

"How much?" she asked.

"Between five and ten thousand."

Rheanna winced. That was a lot of money, and they were barely managing as it was. If only this had happened a few weeks later, after the trail ride fundraiser. Assuming they actually pulled the event off.

Was it right to spend so much on one horse that might or might not make it when they had so many others they couldn't afford to care for?

"Any chance you can cut us a deal?" Dave voiced the question she'd been too afraid to, especially after all the unpaid hours the vet had already spent at the ranch.

"Some, maybe." The vet's gaze faltered. "I'm in the red this month."

Likely in part thanks to them. She hated that she'd put him in that position, that they had to have this conversation at all. And yet, what was the alternative? To let all these horses die? She couldn't. Nor could she give up on Asha.

Amelia would be crushed.

But Rheanna had already tapped her savings dry and her credit card was nearly maxed.

"We'll figure it out." Dave gave her hand a quick squeeze. "You do what you need to, Doc."

She studied his face, trying to find calm from his confidence. "How?"

"Like I said, we'll figure something out. I'll figure something out. If the ranch can't fund the vet bills, then I will."

"I can't let you do that."

His gaze hardened with determination. "No offense, Rheanna, but you can't stop me. I've already lost one pregnant broodmare, a sweet gal I never should've bred in the first place. I'm not looking to lose another."

As his eyes, strong and steady, latched onto hers, she felt less alone.

And more drawn to him than ever.

This could be bad, leading her into yet another heartache.

After how long it'd taken her to get over Dave the first time, she knew better than to entertain a do-over. Regardless of how her rebellious and foolish heart might be trying to lead her.

The vet gathered his things. "Let me deposit my bag in my rig. Then, Dave, maybe you can help me load this gal in."

Dave nodded.

When Wallow returned, he led Asha by the halter. Dave took her tail to help her balance while Rheanna followed, wringing her hands. She knew going into ranching she'd have to deal with sick and wounded animals. But she hadn't anticipated the emotional toll this would take. The attachment she'd feel for each horse.

Asha loaded, she and Dave stood, side by side, watching the trailer drive away until even the dust billowing behind it had settled.

Her eyes stung with the threat of tears. Over a decade ago, her uncle had driven Bella away in a similar trailer, only Bella had been dead.

Gone, in what had felt like an instant.

The day before, Rheanna had been riding her horse across the open range, dreaming of competing in shows. Of learning to jump together, her, her horse and Dave. The next morning, her uncle had woken her with the news. She'd been so distraught. Once her sobs had subsided enough for her to catch her breath, she'd gone to Dave's, seeking comfort. But he'd acted strange. Distant. Like he was merely saying all the things he thought she might need to hear. Almost like his words had been forced or something.

He and his family had moved not long after.

Dave came to her side. "You okay?"

She nodded.

He took her hand and twined his fingers in hers. "I'm here."

And for now, he was.

Chapter Eleven

Phone in hand, Dave paced the length of his small kitchen.

He'd already basically lost his ranch and home. Who knew how long it'd take to recover, or if he could survive financially waiting for new pasture to grow?

And now he was about to sell off most of his remaining herd.

To keep one mare and her fetus alive.

And to help Rheanna. After what happened with Bella, he owed her that much. Besides, he couldn't do nothing. He wouldn't be yet one more person in Asha's life who abandoned her.

How much of his actions were tied up with all he'd experienced here, at this ranch? The hope, the loss? When they'd packed up their cabin that day, he'd thought for certain his parents would send him off, just like so many of his other placements had. Folks seemed quick to take a kid in, make all sorts of promises, until things became inconvenient.

Granted, his behavior had usually caused the inconvenience, but Asha's? This wasn't her fault, and he'd promised to take care of her. Promised her a better life. Though she couldn't understand his words, he was certain she read his heart.

More than that, somehow, as she showed the first signs of trust, started to heal, so did he.

Somehow to lose her, he'd be losing a piece of himself.

With a deep breath, he clicked the dial icon, then waited for his friend to pick up.

"Dave. Good to hear from you." Machinery hummed in the background.

His friend sounded hopeful. "Still don't have an answer on that business proposition, unfortunately." Not just because of his ranch, but also because the thought of leaving here, of leaving Rheanna, felt heavier by the day. He was beginning to realize he'd never truly gotten over her. He'd simply shoved his feelings for her down. But here, working with her every day, looking into her eyes, watching her tenderness with Amelia or the horses, reminded him of who she was.

A woman he wasn't ready to leave.

Mitch released a breath.

Dave poured himself a glass of milk. "You need an answer now?"

"I was hoping for one soon. I mean, I'd love to do this with you. You're my first choice. But if you can't—"

"You've got to find someone else. I get it."

"How are those horses looking?"

"Better. Not 100 percent out of the woods yet, but better." Who would step in once he left? There was no way Rheanna would have the funds to pay for everything she needed. Had she received any bites on those ads he'd placed? Maybe if she got the right trainer in, increased her lessons, filled up all her empty stalls with boarders.

"You looking to add more females to your herd?"

His friend didn't answer right away. "It's come to that?"

"Guess it has." He could bounce back from that. So long as he kept his land and enough horses to breed.

"I suppose if we do end up going into business together, they'll be yours again anyway. In that case, this would be more like a loan. How many were you looking to sell?"

"Here's the deal." He explained how much he needed and why.

"If you're in a bind, another Realtor, this one from Denver, has been poking around."

His stomach clenched at the thought. He'd assumed, partnering with his friend, he could keep his land. His and Mitch's property sat close enough. His ranch would probably fall under both of their names, sure, but that didn't bother him. It'd still be his. Something he'd worked hard to buy and build, and something he still retained.

To sell?

That'd kill his dad. Waste the hard-earned money he'd invested in Dave. Worse, prove his confidence had been misplaced. "If I get that desperate, I'll call you."

What if he paid for Asha's surgery, risked his ranch to help save Rheanna's, and the IRS came and seized it all?

But what if Dave was holding on to something God was leading him from? If so, then to where? To partnering with his friend or staying here, with Rheanna.

Would she want him to? Not just for what he could do on the ranch, for the horses, but for him?

If not, could he still stay?

That'd tear him up.

Common sense told him to get out now, while his heart was still intact. But she couldn't fight this battle alone. Not with how little she understood of the business side of things. As far as he could tell, Bill wasn't helping much. He probably wanted to see her fail, see this property go to auction so he could buy it out from under her.

If she'd been anyone else, he might've said she deserved it, with how her uncle had treated his family. But
she wasn't just some slimy landowner's niece.

She was Rheanna. The woman he'd once loved.

If he were honest, the only woman, other than his mom,
that he'd allowed himself to love.

And look how that had turned out. Yet he was here now.

For good reason, because God always had good reason. Whether that meant anything happening between
him and Rheanna, he didn't know. But he did know God
had good planned.

Maybe, in helping to save the ranch, he could finally
move past the guilt he carried regarding Bella.

And maybe, in helping to save Asha, his heart could
heal from all the grief and guilt he carried from the flood.

If she died and Rheanna lost her ranch, and these
horses? Would he carry the burden of that, too?

He checked the time. He could fit in cleaning one more
stall before he needed to meander to the arena.

He'd just made it back from the compost pile when his
phone rang. It was his student, canceling, which cut his
paycheck but provided just over an hour of "free time."
Though there was always extra work to tackle, the homeschooled triplets would be out later and could take care
of most of it.

That meant he could help Rheanna untangle her uncle's ledgers.

Rheanna trimmed her basil plants, hoping to increase
the yield. She shielded her eyes from the sun and surveyed
the rest of her garden. Their cilantro, beets and carrots
were thriving. Plenty for a nice salad.

Her phone buzzed in her back pocket, sending a jolt of

adrenaline through her. She glanced at the screen and answered. "Dave, hi. Is something wrong? Did the vet call?"

"Nothing yet. I'm at your house. Wondered if now would be a good time for me to help you with your paperwork."

"Sure." She stood and dusted the dirt from the back of her pants. "I could use the distraction." Her mind refused to settle, jumping from the mare, her daughter, the ranch, her problems with the IRS, to Dave and all the emotions he stirred within her. It was all too much to process.

"I get that. But everything's going to work out. I believe that."

She never knew how much of what he said portrayed genuine confidence or was meant to reassure her. Either way, she appreciated his steady strength. "There's lemonade in the fridge and some fresh baked muffins on the counter."

"Did Ivy bake them?"

His hesitant tone made her smile. "Maybe."

"Oh, joy."

She laughed. "Help yourself. I'll be there in a moment."

When she reached her house, she found Dave sitting in the rocker on the porch, sipping from a water bottle. "You should've gone inside and out of the sun." T-Bone lay stretched out at his feet, head on his foreleg.

"I was just hanging out with my buddy here, wasn't I, boy?" He reached down to scratch the dog's head, then stood as Rheanna climbed the steps.

She deposited her pail, gloves and garden shovel beside the welcome mat, then stepped inside, holding the door open for him. The cool air soothed her hot, itchy skin and sent a delicious shiver down her spine.

"I'll grab us something to drink." She hurried into the kitchen and paused to orient herself.

Whatever emotional distance their years apart had created had now vanished completely, leaving her feeling more vulnerable than ever.

But she had a child to raise, a ranch to run and tax issues to solve, which meant she needed to keep her wits about her. With a huff, she pulled two glasses from the cupboard, lemonade from the fridge and reached for the plate of muffins Ivy had made.

She suppressed a giggle remembering Dave's less than enthused tone when they'd spoken by phone, and the way he grimaced whenever sampling Ivy's "treats." No offense to her friend, but like Amelia said, those muffins needed gluten. And sugar. And maybe a little less protein powder.

She grabbed her secret stash of chewy fudge chocolate chip cookies hidden behind the china they never used, poured them onto a plate, and strode back into the living room. Dave stood in the same place she'd left him, with one hand in his pocket.

"Have one." She held the plate out to him. "They're full of gluten, sugar, hydrogenized oil and more preservatives than a leather factory."

His smile crinkled the skin around his eyes. "If you put it that way." He eyed the mounds of paper scattered across the dining table. "This is it, huh?"

"Hopefully, though my uncle didn't exactly keep everything in one place. Still, I doubt he's entirely to blame. I don't know when he stopped managing the finances himself. I see at least two different handwriting styles that indicate he had others handling his books for him."

He gave a slow nod. "Where's the IRS letter?"

She gave it to him, and he pulled on the skin beneath his chin as he read it. "What all have you been able to gather?"

"Here are my uncle's ledgers, but I'm warning you, they're a mess. I ended up creating an Excel spreadsheet."

She opened her laptop and rotated it to face him. "The rows highlighted pink correlate to checked-off entries in the book. The ones highlighted green weren't recorded, as far as I can tell."

Her phone's alarm chimed, and she glanced at the screen. "I'm so sorry, but I need to go. Lucy and I are meeting with Mr. and Mrs. Hayes to, hopefully, convince them to let us use their land, free of charge, for the trail ride." She had hoped to get more done while Amelia was at day camp. Seemed she never had enough time to tackle all she needed to.

"Inviting the missus. Smart."

She nodded. "And Lucy's bringing in a reinforcement— her famous cinnamon streusel coffee cake."

"With gluten?" Laughter danced in his eyes.

"Massive amounts." She smiled. "Along with a gift card to Tabitha's salon, which she generously donated, for extra measure."

He raised his eyebrows. "Sounds to me like you've got this in the bag."

"Hopefully. Then afterward, I'm meeting with Walt Milton—"

His eyes widened at the mention of her uncle's former ranch manager, then narrowed as a flash of contempt darkened his expression. His odd reaction once again stirred questions she felt she didn't have the right to ask. She suspected whatever had occurred between Dave, his family and her uncle was none of her business, and she didn't like to pry.

Her gaze shifted back to the IRS letter, lying faceup, smack-dab in the middle of her paper mess, and she slumped.

He must've noticed, because he stood and grabbed her shoulders so that she was forced to look into his light brown eyes.

"We'll get through this."

We'll. As if they were a pair.

Which they weren't. She straightened and took a step back. "Call me if anything changes with Asha?"

"Will do."

Then, with one last glance at the piles covering that table, she grabbed her purse and left.

When she arrived at Wilma's, she wasn't surprised to find Lucy already waiting in a booth near the back. Dressed down from her normal preppy attire, she wore a teal T-shirt, jean Bermudas and hiking sandals. Apparently, she'd also left her thick file of notes, which she normally brought to every trail-related meeting, at home. But based on the wrapped box sitting on the table, she'd remembered the dessert.

Saying hello to Trinity Faith friends in passing, Rheanna hurried across the dining room and greeted the woman who had become her greatest supporter in Sage Creek with a hug. "Thank you so much for coming." She slid into the booth beside her.

"You didn't think I'd let you dance with the bear all by yourself, did you? I'd never miss out on that kind of entertainment." She winked, then patted Rheanna's hand. "Don't worry. I suspect his wife will soften him up plenty."

"One can hope."

They soon discovered, however, that wasn't the case. If anything, Mrs. Hayes's presence only made her husband gruffer as they talked through the trail ride project and other ranchers' willingness to help. Though his scowl and tense posture relaxed some once he opened the cake box.

He studied Lucy. "What's this?"

"Just a little something to thank you for your time."

Her response seemed to momentarily steal his words.

But then, with a brisk nod, he grabbed the box and said to his wife, "Let's go."

Rheanna watched them leave, trying to gauge the effectiveness of their meeting. She turned back to Lucy. "Well?"

Her friend deposited a twenty-dollar bill on the table. "Progress, my friend." She checked her phone screen. "You free this afternoon for some window-shopping? I need to find a giveaway gift for this weekend's bunco night."

"I wish I could, but I've got some other unpleasant business to attend to."

"Care to talk about it?"

"Honestly, I'd rather forget the whole mess entirely. But considering I can't do that…" She told her about her next meeting with her uncle's former ranch manager.

"God will work it all out. Trust Him."

She wanted to, but her experience showed things often didn't turn out how one hoped, regardless of how many desperate prayers a person offered.

Lucy gave her a hug, promised to pray for her, then left.

Rheanna remained, sipping her now-cold coffee while obsessively checking the time on her cell. She was just about to leave when Walt Milton sauntered in with his jaw set and chin raised.

Almost like he was preparing for a battle.

Rheanna stood when he reached her table. "Thanks for meeting with me." She offered her hand, but he ignored her and sat.

He leaned back, arms crossed. "Don't have much time."

"I understand." She started to explain her IRS troubles, but stopped when Sally Jo came over with her notepad. She waited until Walt had placed his order—which she was going to have to pay for, obviously—before continuing.

He took a slow swig of water, then set his glass down with a thud. "And I can help you how?"

"I assume you managed the books?"

"Some."

"Can you help me make sense of it all?" She flipped open a file folder containing copied documents. "Specifically these expenses? I need to find a way to prove their validity as tax deductions."

He scratched his jaw. "Can't say that I remember those. I managed a lot of transactions for your uncle. We all did."

"You're saying everyone had their hands in the bookkeeping?"

"Don't know about everyone, but a few."

No wonder it was all such a disaster.

"If you remember anything about these expenses or where I might find more detailed information, will you call me?"

"Sure enough."

By then his food had come, and their conversation abruptly ended. Not that the man had been hugely talkative or helpful prior.

Now what?

Walt finished his last bite, swiped a napkin across his mouth, crumpled it and tossed it on his plate. "Thanks for the meal."

She nodded, feeling like she'd just wasted ten bucks.

After he left, she sat for some time, fighting her catapulting thoughts. What if she'd never come to Sage Creek? What if she'd kept her job and apartment back home?

And had never reconnected with Dave and experienced all the emotions their reunion triggered. Of everything she was struggling to process, she found his presence and the war raging in her heart the most frightening.

The loneliness she'd often battled prior to moving to Sage Creek had been nothing compared to the gaping wound she'd suffered once he'd left all those years ago.

The sound of someone clearing his throat beside her grabbed her attention. She looked up to see an older man with a thick, unkempt beard and bushy eyebrows standing beside her.

"Don't mean to stick my nose where it don't belong," he said. "But that Walt is one shady character. Word has it, he swindled more than a few horse buyers, enough where folks won't let him into auctions anymore."

"How?"

"Failing to disclose vet bills and behavioral issues. Promising a bill of sale folks never got. Course, no one's been able to prove outright malice. But I wouldn't be surprised if he fiddled with tax stuff."

If what this man said was true, the ranch had earned a horrible reputation, one that wouldn't be easy to change. No wonder she couldn't get people to board with her. "In other words, I likely owe the IRS a lot of money."

He shrugged, tipped his hat and ambled off, leaving Rheanna feeling more discouraged and overwhelmed than ever.

Chapter Twelve

Once again, Dave found himself at Rheanna's house, going through old documents. Receipts and invoices from ten years ago were intermixed with more current ones, almost as if someone had intentionally jumbled it all. Then again, after how Mr. Green had treated Dave's parents, this wouldn't surprise him. That man hadn't had a bone of integrity in his body.

Dave stood, stretched, then grabbed an old, rubber-banded shoebox near his feet. He set it on the table and began going through it. What he read halfway through stopped him. Cincinnati Children's Hospital Medical Center Oncology. Rheanna's maiden name appeared on the line denoting patient. According to the date, she'd gone in for treatment shortly after her uncle had given Dave and his family the boot.

Selling the land out from under them for… He flipped through more pages, totaling numbers in his mind… The cost of cancer treatment? Could that be what had caused Mr. Green to act so underhandedly, and so unexpectedly?

Did Rheanna know? Surely she would've said something.

Her world must've been turned upside down. Based on

what he knew about her mother, the poor girl had likely endured much of her battle alone.

I should've been there for her.

So convinced she'd rejected him, so caught up in his own drama, he'd given up far too easily.

And what about her actions afterward? Her failure to return his letters—assuming she even received them. Had she just been too worn-out from treatment, needing to be alone? He'd judged her for her silence. Now he judged himself for lacking patience and sympathy. But he was here now, and maybe this was why. Maybe his leaving back then had hurt her even more deeply than it'd hurt him. Was God giving them both the chance to try again? To hold tight to one another, no matter what?

The front door burst open, slamming against the wall with a thud, as a rosy-cheeked, bright-eyed Amelia ran in. "With whip cream and sprinkles?"

Rheanna followed a couple of steps behind. "Of course. What's a milkshake without whipped cream and sprinkles?"

Upon seeing Dave, the smile in her eyes deepened, sending a wave of warmth through him. Her sweet beauty captivated him, even more so now, after all he knew.

Cancer. To think, he could've lost her, like really lost her. But she was okay now, right?

What about that doctor's appointment she'd had in Houston? He tried to recall her behavior before and after for evidence of her mood.

She closed the door behind her, then turned to Dave. "Any luck?"

He repositioned the lid on the shoebox and placed it back at his feet. "Not really." Should he ask her about the cancer? Did he even have a right to? Maybe, but not now. Not in front of Amelia.

"Mama's taking me to Wilma's." Amelia twirled, her braids swinging about her head, then skipped to his side. "On account I was so good and helpful and kind."

"Really?" He gave her a high five. "That's awesome."

Rheanna nodded. "Her Bible teacher gave her a prize for showing compassion. She stuck up for one of the other kids who was getting bullied."

"Way to go, kiddo." He ruffled her hair. "That was very brave."

She shrugged. "I've been bullied before. It made me really sad, and no one helped me. Not even my best friend. Well, she used to be my best friend, but then she started acting stupid and mean."

"I'm sorry to hear that."

"I've got friends now." Her wide grin returned. "Wanna come with us?"

"To Wilma's?" His gaze shot to Rheanna, who appeared flustered by the question.

She smoothed a hand over Amelia's head. "I'm sure Mister Dave has plenty to do this afternoon."

"Ah." Amelia slumped. "Like what? Do you have lessons?"

He checked the time on his phone. It was only one thirty. "Actually, I'm free until four."

"Yay!" Amelia bounced on her feet. "Then you can come. Right, Mama?"

Rheanna's cheeks blossomed the most adorable pink, and her eyes searched his, as if trying to gauge his interest level. He wasn't sure he wanted that to show just yet. Then again, if he didn't tell her how he felt, he might lose her for good, and he wasn't sure he wanted to do that, either.

Rheanna's phone rang before she could respond. She glanced at her screen and visibly stiffened. "Hello?" Pausing, she released a breath that ended in something of a laugh. "That's great news." She shot Dave a grin. "Yes, of course. I understand."

When she hung up, the hope in her eyes was evident— and contagious.

"And?" His chest felt tight.

"That was Doc Wallow. Mother and baby survived surgery."

He released the breath he'd been holding. "I knew Asha was a fighter. And that God didn't bring her and her foal to us just so they could die."

"They're going to be okay? Mama?" Amelia tugged on Rheanna's arm. "Mama, is Asha going to be okay?"

Rheanna dropped to one knee and drew her daughter to her. She appeared to be struggling with what to say, or maybe with how honest to be regarding the uncertainties ahead. "They're both doing well and are receiving the best care possible. But he wants to keep Asha at his clinic for a while, so he can watch her and her unborn foal. They're not out of the woods yet, sweetie."

Tiny lines etched across Amelia's forehead, but then she raised her chin. "We should tell Jesus. He'll fix them."

The steady, unquestioning faith of a child.

Rheanna gave a gentle smile. "That's a great idea."

They'd barely circled up, hand in hand, when Amelia launched into the sweetest, purest, most precious prayer Dave had heard.

Please, Lord, don't let her down.

The girl would be doubly crushed, first at losing the horses, then by the sting of shattered faith.

Unfortunately, he understood what both felt like.

A sense of sacredness, made all the heavier by the weight of the situation, filled the room, at least, for a moment, until Amelia's cheerful yet dogged petitions resumed.

"Mama, you never answered my question about Mister Dave. Can he come? Can he? Can he? Can he?"

Rheanna blinked a few times before offering a smooth smile. "Of course, dear. If he wants."

"Do you, Mister Dave? They have chocolate and vanilla and strawberry and will add fancy sugar and sprinkles on top, if you ask them to."

He laughed at her enthusiasm, then sobered as his gaze shifted to Rheanna. "I would love to come."

He was treading on dangerous terrain, heading heart-first in a direction logic told him to avoid. But his heart wasn't listening any more today than it had nearly two decades ago. And if he landed in the same place? There'd been a time when that question, the threat of hurt, would've sent him running in the other direction. But now, standing here, looking into Rheanna's deep brown eyes, an even more powerful question arose: What if he walked away from his chance at love?

A small, warm hand grabbed hold of his, reminding him that, should things not work out between him and Rheanna, he wasn't the only one who'd get hurt.

He and Rheanna needed to talk. Figure out where they stood, where they wanted to stand.

But not today. This afternoon's outing was about the sweet little princess inviting him for ice cream.

Apparently, they weren't moving fast enough, because Amelia grabbed both their hands and pulled them toward the door. "Come on." She beamed up first at Rheanna then at him.

As if the three of them were a happy little family.

Could they be?

After their treat at the diner, Rheanna helped Amelia out of Dave's truck and unlatched her booster seat.

She smiled at him. "Thanks for this afternoon. I can't remember the last time I enjoyed a root beer float."

"Guess we should do it again sometime, huh?"

"Yeah!" Amelia darted to Rheanna's side and poked her face between her mom and the door. "Can we? Tomorrow? Or maybe the day after?"

Rheanna laughed. "Sugar two days in a row?"

"Or the park. We could have a picnic. You, me and Mister Dave."

Rheanna frowned and dropped her gaze. Amelia was getting used to this, the three of them together. Getting used to having Dave around.

She was going to be crushed when he left.

And if he stayed? What made her think he'd give up his land, for her?

That wouldn't even be fair for her to ask. And besides, if he did and her ranch failed, he'd resent her. That would hurt even worse than losing him.

Rheanna thanked Dave again, closed the door, then deposited Amelia's booster on the porch and followed Amelia into the house.

Ivy was in the kitchen as usual, expensive baking supplies strewn all over.

"Hey, there." She swiped hair from her face with the back of her hand, leaving a streak of some sort of white substance on her forehead. "What's up?"

Rheanna opened the fridge. Nearly empty, and it was Ivy's turn to buy the groceries. Just like it'd been her turn to fill up the gas tank, only she hadn't done that, either.

Rheanna sat. "Can we talk?"

"Sure." She joined Rheanna at the table, their chairs angled toward one another. "Everything okay with Asha?"

"We're hopeful." She relayed what the vet had told her.

"Wow. Did he say how much that'll cost?"

"A lot." Rheanna picked at a cuticle. She'd never enjoyed conflict, plus she felt a little guilty initiating this conversation, considering all Ivy had done for her. Maybe not financially, but emotionally, she'd stood beside her when it felt like her world had been crashing in. She'd helped Rheanna pick herself back up, learn to dream again.

Find the courage to come here in the first place.

She released a breath. "We're not making budget."

Ivy nodded. "Expenses have been crazy, huh?"

"They have. I need to be more…careful with how I spend my money."

"Okay? So, like, you're thinking of getting rid of the rescues?"

"What?" She coughed the word out. "No. Why would I do that?"

"You said you're short on cash. I figured—"

"I can't keep funding your business."

Ivy jerked back. "My bus—" She huffed. "We knew it'd take time to turn a profit. Besides, we're in this together. Remember?"

"I need to focus on the ranch. Otherwise I'll lose it." She might anyway. Then what? Would she be out a friend, too? Hopefully not. Their friendship was strong enough to carry hard conversations. Wasn't it?

"What are you saying? You want me to leave?"

"No. But I need you to contribute more."

"How am I supposed to do that?"

"For starters, you can help more on the ranch."

"I already do."

"Not enough."

She scoffed. "I get it. You want me to give up my dream for yours."

"Just spend less time and money pursuing it."

"Clearly you have zero understanding of what it takes to become a successful entrepreneur."

"You've become obsessed, Ivy. Look, I know—"

"Stop." She held up her hand. "You've said your piece. Obviously, our ideas of doing life together, as you yourself call it, are different." She started to stand, then sat back down, her mood swinging a few notches from high dudgeon to mere irritation. "I've been wanting to talk to you about our arrangement but didn't want to hurt your feelings. Might as well be direct, right?"

"Okay?"

"Sage Creek isn't working for me or my business. They've got one coffeehouse/bakery, a tiny grocery with a nearly nonexistent health food section and a diner that specializes in fried chicken."

"What are you saying?"

"I'm saying, maybe it's time you and I part ways."

"Where will you go?"

"Austin."

"How will you afford that?"

"I've met someone."

That explained her increasingly frequent trips.

"He's part owner of a trendy little restaurant, in fact. What's more, he loves my products and wants to link arms. And you know what? I need that. Someone who actually believes in me and what I'm trying to do."

"Ivy—"

She shook her head and stood. "I'm done. So done." Shaking her head, she stormed out of the kitchen.

Rheanna blinked back tears. Done from what? The ranch or their friendship?

She closed her eyes and rubbed her face.

What had just happened? Ivy had never behaved so irrationally before. Then again, if what she said was true, it appeared her discontent, and perhaps even resentment toward Rheanna for bringing her here, had been building for some time.

If Rheanna had known all that coming to Sage Creek would cost, she would've legally disclaimed the inheritance. But she thought it had offered her—and Ivy—a fresh start. A chance to raise her daughter in the country with a close-knit community.

And she had that. She had all the ladies at Trinity Faith, Lucy and Doris and their sweet friends. But she still felt alone, because she'd lost the one person she thought she could always rely on.

Again.

It seemed everyone she'd ever depended on left eventually. The dad who never wanted her. The mom who'd continually pushed her aside whenever a new man started coming around. Her ex-husband, and now Ivy.

Her mind jumped to Dave. She still had him. But for how long?

She needed air. With a huff, she grabbed her water bottle, filled it and strode into the living room.

Amelia lay sprawled on the floor coloring.

"Mommy's going to go check on the horses," Rheanna said. "You be good. Watch some TV, if you want."

"Can I come?"

"Not this time, sweetie." Normally she loved having her daughter with her, but tonight she needed time to process.

This was all feeling much too similar to how she'd felt back when Bella had died. The summer she'd lost both her best friends, the horse and Dave.

She was so very tired of being alone.

Outside, the air was hot, muggy and carried the scent of rain. The breeze swept the aroma of hay, earth and wildflowers as she stalked down the gravel road toward the trails they were restoring. She pounded her emotions into the dirt with every step.

She'd spent so many afternoons in those trees, finding solace in the snap of branches as squirrels scampered about. Listening to birds chirp or the wind rustle the leaves. Listening to Dave crack some joke or other. Somehow, he'd always known where to find her.

He'd always known just when she'd needed finding.

"Hey, there." Heavy boots crunched on the gravel behind her, rapidly approaching. Upon reaching her, Dave grabbed her arm. "What's up?"

She turned to face him.

"What's going on?" Eyes searching hers, he brushed a lock of hair from her face, his knuckle lingering near her chin.

"I don't want to talk about it." Because if she did, she might cry.

"Is it Asha?"

She shook her head, tears pricking at the thought, at knowing she could get a call any minute letting her know the mare, foal or both had taken an unexpected turn for the worst.

"Then what? An angry phone call from a boarder?"

"Life. That's what. My life." She turned and resumed walking.

He matched her steps. "Want to talk?"

She increased her pace.

Dave didn't push, but neither did he leave.

Breath labored, she slowed once they entered the woods, eyes set on the trail in front of her. How could she verbalize all that was in her heart, all the questions swirling through her mind? The ache of knowing, come summer's end, Dave would likely be gone, too?

They continued in silence until they reached the edge of the property, bordering Mr. Reynolds's land.

Back when they'd been kids, they came here often, scooting under the barbed wire and continuing on to a patch of pasture dotted with towering blackberry bushes. Then, lying shoulder to shoulder on the ground, they'd talk. Sometimes they'd just lie there, watching the clouds drift by.

She stopped and plucked a leaf from a nearby tree. "Ivy's leaving."

"I'm sorry."

"Honestly, it's probably for the best. Coming here changed her, or maybe brought out a previously dormant part of her. Although I'm not one to walk away from friendships so easily, she's not happy here. I've known that for some time."

She sat at the tree's base and leaned against its trunk.

He hovered over her for a moment, and she could feel him watching her. But she didn't look up, because if she made eye contact, if she saw the same depth of love that she'd always seen there when they'd been kids, she'd become a sobbing mess.

With an audible breath, he sat beside her, his arm lightly brushing hers, filling her nose with his familiar scent of hay, musky aftershave and leather.

She pulled her legs to her chest and rested her chin on her knees. "I feel like it's all falling apart." She told him about her meeting with Walt Milton and the conversation with a rancher that followed. "I likely owe every penny, money I don't have. I don't even want to see the vet bills, once Dr. Wallow releases Asha."

"I'll pay for that."

She angled her head with a frown. "How? Because

last I remember, you weren't exactly in the best state financially."

He winced and looked away briefly. "I'm doing well enough. Let me help you. Lean on me, Rhe."

She wanted to trust him, to believe that he truly would stand beside her in this, and for a thousand hard moments to follow. But letting him in now would only make it hurt all the more once he left. "You'll be gone soon enough."

Finger under her chin, he angled her head so her gaze met his once again. "I don't have to be."

The back of her throat burned. "What are you saying?"

"I'm asking if you'd like me to stay."

"To help with the ranch?"

He blinked, as if her words had hurt him. "Do you want more?"

And if she said yes? If she opened her heart to this man, this man who had left, but who'd returned. Who was here now. "Do you?"

He swallowed, nodded and ran the pad of his thumb across her bottom lip. "I do."

"What about Amelia? Because I'm a package deal."

"I recognize that."

That was what worried her most. She knew he meant well, but did he truly want to be a father? And a father of a child that wasn't his? This wasn't like playing house.

Was he prepared for the late nights soothing a sick child? The temper tantrums she sometimes threw when she became overtired? The frustration of asking her to do the same thing for the hundredth time, only to find it didn't get done?

The hard, sometimes dirty, often confusing stuff of parenting?

The day-to-day difficulties her ex-husband, obviously, hadn't had time for.

"Give me a chance? That's all I'm asking."

She stared into his eyes, wanting so badly to believe this was real, that this was true.

To trust him fully with her heart. As she once had.

"Come here." He placed an arm around her.

She stiffened, ready to push him away. But then she took a deep breath and rested her head against his shoulder and cried.

She cried for Asha and all the uncertainties surrounding her. For the ranch and the debt they owed. For the friendship she may have lost for good.

And for this. The love she'd lost that, though her heart wanted to believe they could find again, her head worried they had too many things standing in their way. Life wasn't nearly as simple as it had been when they were kids.

"I'm here, Rhe." Lifting her chin, he turned her face toward him and thumbed away a tear. "I'm here."

Her breath hitched as he leaned closer and kissed her.

Chapter Thirteen

Amelia burst into the house with windblown hair. "Mama! Come help me train Opie."

"But he's so well-behaved already."

"Not to ride, silly. To read. I want to do a show like that horse Mister Dave told us about. Remember? The one that learned to read and add his numbers. Come on. Mister Dave is waiting."

A warmth swept through her as she remembered his kiss. And his promise to stick around. Only his statement hadn't been that committed, had it? He'd asked her to give them a chance.

"Mama, come on."

"All right. All right." Laughing, she followed after her daughter, arriving at the lesson stables breathless, and not merely because of her jog there.

Dave hung a halter on a hook. "Our little teacher roped you into helping, too, huh?"

"Looks like it." Something she wasn't unhappy about, despite her desire to proceed with caution.

Amelia plopped onto the ground next to her rusted lunch pail, a grimy book bag and a mound of wrapped peppermint likely snatched from the tack room. "We'll do counting first."

"Okay." Dave looked at Amelia with the seriousness a vet might display explaining medication doses, and Rheanna loved him for it.

Amelia pulled hand-drawn cards from her bag. "Can I teach Asha's baby, once she's born?"

Rheanna smiled. "I don't see why not."

Dave nodded. "In fact, if your mama says it's okay, you can help me train her. Get her used to people and what not."

"Yay! I can be her aunty. Can I use some of your printer paper, Mama?"

"Yes, but what for?"

"To make the baby a birthday card." She turned to Dave. "We can make another cake, like we did for Mama."

Rheanna's heart swelled at the memory of the three of them on Dave's porch, acting like a family. What would it be like to have someone like Dave, someone so kind and patient, with the same steady strength, to rely on? What would it be like for Amelia to have a daddy—a man who actually stuck around?

Dave's gaze captured and held hers, and she made no attempt to look away.

Dave Brewster, can we trust you with our hearts?

"You're not listening!" Amelia slapped her hand on the ground.

Rheanna's eyebrows shot up. She suppressed a laugh. "Sorry, sweetie. What were you saying?"

"I'm telling you how to use the flash cards."

"Oh, of course." She straightened, attempting to look as serious as possible.

After relaying detailed instructions, Amelia marched

them to Opie's stall, where she displayed her notecards one by one. "This is an *A*, and it makes an *ah* sound."

Unfortunately, the horse was more interested in hay than lessons.

Amelia crossed her arms. "He's not paying attention."

"I've got an idea." Dave's eyes twinkled with amusement.

Her pout lessened. "Okay."

"How about we tape two letter cards on the wall and hold the peppermint to the correct one. Then maybe Opie will associate touching his nose to it with getting candy."

Rheanna stepped back, watching the two interact. She'd long wished for a daddy figure for Amelia. What if God was answering Rheanna's prayers in bringing Dave into their lives?

Her phone rang. She glanced at the screen before answering. "Bill, hi."

"Mrs. Hayes is here to see you."

"Did she say why?"

"Nope. Just that she needs to talk with you directly."

Hopefully to share good news. "I'll be right there." Call ended, she faced the teacher duo. "Sorry, but I've got to go. Can we do this again?"

Eyes bright, Amelia nodded.

Dave's gaze intensified. "I'd enjoy that."

She would, too, and it scared her just how much. "Thank you. For the rain check and..." *Making my girl feel special. Stepping into the void her biological father left. For helping me feel less alone.*

Outside the house, Mrs. Hayes was sitting in her truck, engine running, horse trailer attached to her vehicle. Odd.

She stepped out as Rheanna approached. "Hi." She looked nervous, not a good sign.

"Ma'am. How can I help you?"

"Do you have a minute?"

"Have a seat on the porch. I'll bring us some lemonade." She strode inside and returned with a tray of drinks and cranberry biscuits left over from breakfast. "Everything all right?"

Mrs. Hayes sat in a rocker. "I have a proposition I think would help us both."

"Okay."

"I brought my horse, Marigold." She wrapped both hands around her glass. "She's got Equine Proto-whatever—EPM."

Rheanna stifled a gasp. "Are you sure?" Equine Protozoal Myeloencephalitis could be a long-term illness. Even after drug therapy, a horse wouldn't recover what it had lost to the parasite, and the symptoms could return later, triggering more treatment.

"The vet came out this morning."

"Is she being treated?"

She nodded. "We'd like to board her here in exchange for access to our property. For your trail ride event." Her faltering gaze suggested this arrangement wouldn't be temporary.

She was passing off her "damaged" horse. While not a danger to the rest of her herd, the mare would likely need ongoing treatment—without a guaranteed outcome. The expense could cost much more than anything Rheanna might've paid for use of the Hayes's land. Still, she couldn't turn Marigold away. What if they decided to put her down?

Rheanna wouldn't let that happen.

She offered her most reassuring smile and stood. "Let's get your girl settled."

Mrs. Hayes visibly relaxed. "Thank you."

Once Marigold was secure in a freshly cleaned stall and

Mrs. Hayes had left, Rheanna contacted her vet, asking him to call her back. She returned to her rocker and stared toward the distant trees, feeling the full weight of all she'd taken on with the ranch. At some point, Amelia whizzed by, chattering about needing more markers, and barged inside. Dave followed and stopped at the porch steps.

Concern radiated from his eyes. "Hey." He sat beside her. "You all right?"

Fighting tears, she shook her head and relayed all that had happened. "I know this horse will only add to our expenses, but I didn't know what else to do."

"You made the right choice." He placed his hand, warm and strong, over hers. "Like I told you before, God's got this. Got you and Amelia, too."

"I'm going to have to concede to the IRS. I'm pretty sure those expenses weren't legit, and that they weren't the only false claims made. The longer I try to untangle it all, the more interest I'll have to pay. I'm going to have to have an accountant look it all over, but I'm sure it won't be good news."

He stared at his hands for a moment, rubbing at his thumb knuckle, then stood. "Let me see what I can do." He left before she could ask what he meant. Honestly, she was afraid to, for fear of shattering the little hope his words created.

Although she didn't know what he had planned, she knew he wouldn't give up until he figured something out. Because that was the kind of man he was.

Dave Brewster, what would we do without you?

She'd never thought a truer question, and that terrified her. If experience had taught her anything, it was to never rely on a man.

But Dave was different. Hadn't he shown her that? He was still here, after all.

* * *

When Dave's afternoon student canceled, he decided to use his unexpected free time to visit his parents. He called his buddy from Cheyenne on the way. No sense delaying his decision any longer. He knew, regardless of how things turned out between him and Rheanna, he couldn't leave. She and the ranch needed him, and he now knew God had called him back to Sage Creek to help her, to love on sweet Amelia and to help save the ranch.

Thankfully, his buddy understood. Hopefully Dave's parents would, as well. The thought of causing them pain twisted his gut.

Lord, I believe this is how You're leading me, and I have to believe that means You'll take care of everything and everyone else. That You'll maybe even bring my folks healing through all this. Just like You did for me.

Worried tonight might reopen old wounds, he spent the rest of the drive mentally rehearsing his words.

His mother stepped onto her porch as he pulled into her driveway. She'd cut her hair since he'd seen her last so that her silver locks now hit maybe an inch beneath her pointed chin. She wore jeans and a maroon blouse with short, puffy sleeves.

"Hey." He tipped his hat and climbed the steps.

She pulled him into a tight hug then stepped back. "I've got sweet tea and rhubarb pie, fresh out of the oven, waiting."

He smiled. "You always know how to speak my language." Prior to getting placed with his parents, he assumed women like his mom didn't exist outside of old movies. Then, once he met her, he thought for sure she was putting on an act that would end once her patience ran thin. But she was the real deal and about as motherly as a woman could get.

His dad rose from his recliner to greet Dave with a handshake turned hug. "The drive okay?"

"No problems." Dave set his Stetson on the coffee table and sat across from him, initiating small talk until his mother returned with drinks and ice cream–topped pie.

Dave inched forward to the edge of his seat, elbows on his knees. "I wanted to talk to you about my ranch."

His parents exchanged glances, and his dad nodded for him to continue.

"I want to sell it." He winced at the shock on their faces. He hadn't meant to blurt that out, not like that.

"But that's your dream." Worry lines deepened across his mother's forehead. "I know this is hard. Painful, but don't give up. You've already overcome so very much."

"What I'm asking is, how hurt would you be if I sold?"

His mom started to speak, but his dad raised a hand. "What aren't you telling us?"

He didn't want to add to their pain, but he had to be completely forthright. He owed them that much, and so, beginning with the moment he first returned to Sage Creek, he told them everything.

A thick silence stretched between them, and he could tell his father was fighting a reservoir of emotions.

"Didn't think I'd hear that name again." His father scrubbed a hand over his face. "You thinking of staying on, then?"

"Hoping to." Assuming Rheanna would keep him, but surely with the way she looked at him, the way she'd kissed him the other day, she would. If not? He'd fight for her.

He'd already lost her once. He wasn't looking to do so a second time.

His father's furrowed eyebrows suggested he didn't like Dave's answer. But he didn't try to dissuade him. "Like we've always told you, the strong man forgives, just as the good Lord forgave us. Guess it's time for me to live out my own words." He gave a sad chuckle. "And like you said, the man's dead. We've got nothing against sweet little Rheanna. Then again, she's not so little anymore, is she?"

"Not exactly."

"Her child is," his mom said. "She doesn't deserve to lose her home any more than you did yours."

Dave thought back to the day when he'd watched his mom fight tears as she packed up all their things. He thought for sure that move would break both his parents. He knew now they'd been much too strong for that.

His dad offered a kind smile tinged with a hint of sadness. Or maybe regret. "You do what you feel is right."

"Thanks."

"Now that that's settled…" Mom set her untouched pie on the coffee table. "How about a game of dominoes?"

He laughed. Some things never changed. For that, he was grateful. "One game."

This whole deal had increased his respect for both his parents greatly, if that were even possible. To think, he'd spent the entire drive over stressing about their reaction. He should've known they'd respond in love. They always did.

Dave watched his father clear the coffee table and lay the number tiles on it, like he had so many times when Dave was growing up. No matter what life threw at him, he remained unshakable, demonstrating a quiet strength Dave longed to mimic. He might have lacked father figures growing up. But the dad God gave him more than compensated for the hole Dave's biological father had left.

If Rheanna and Amelia let Dave take on that role, he knew precisely what type of dad he longed to be.

He expected to feel sad at the prospect of selling his

land, or maybe anxious, but he didn't. He felt nothing but peace. Hope, and anticipation when he imagined Rheanna's face once he told her.

Assuming she wanted him to stick around. If she didn't?

Then he'd fight for her. He'd almost lost her once. He wouldn't let that happen again.

And as to her past cancer diagnosis? He'd talk to her about that when God showed him the time was right.

Dusk had started to settle by the time he arrived back at the ranch. Numerous cars were parked outside the main house. A meeting regarding the trail ride?

He might as well check on the rescues while he waited for Rheanna to finish. He'd just brought one of their foals in from pasture when a group of female voices approached. From the sounds of it, Rheanna was giving a tour.

He locked the gate, walked through the stall and out into the aisle with a tip of his hat. "Hello."

His grin froze, then faded. Sally Jo stared back at him from among the women, with that sickly sweet smile of hers. Why was she here? He had a tough time believing it was because she loved horses, or serving for that matter.

"Dave, what a pleasant surprise." Head tilted, she twirled a lock of hair around her finger. "Rheanna here tells us you've been doing an amazing job with these poor creatures. We'd love to hear all about it."

His gaze shot to Rheanna. "Um. Not sure what all I could tell you. Just been following the vet's orders as best as we can."

This led to numerous questions he did his best to answer. Rheanna seemed pleased by the interest, and so she should be. Sally Jo aside, the more people understood all they were doing here, the more they'd feel inclined to help.

"Ladies, we should probably let Dave get back to work."

Rheanna shifted toward the direction from which they'd come. "How about I show you some of our recently repaired trails before it gets dark. Lucy, would you mind leading them that way? I'll catch up momentarily."

Lucy, who he hadn't noticed prior, smiled. "I'd love to."

Rheanna waited until the women were a fair distance away, then turned to Dave. "We lost another boarder tonight. Once they heard about me taking on Marigold."

"You let them know her condition isn't contagious?"

She nodded. "They said they're concerned with 'the direction the ranch is heading.'" She made air quotes. "With my tendency to take on 'sick' animals and what I might be exposing their horse to."

"I'm sorry." How could people be so...presumptuous? Then again, the ranch hadn't exactly been the picture of efficiency and professionalism. But Rheanna was making changes. Couldn't folks see all she was doing and trying to do?

She shrugged. "Like you said earlier, we just need to trust that God's got this."

"He does. I have no doubt." And He was leading Dave to help. He felt certain about that, as well.

He told her about his decision, watching with joy as her eyes widened in surprised delight and relief.

But then she frowned. "I can't let you do that."

"I want to. I care about those horses as much as you do. Besides, I'd probably have to sell my land eventually anyway." If anything, it showed both Dave and Rheanna where Dave's heart was, in a way neither of them could deny. "At least I'll know you won't have to sell yours." Not yet anyway, and hopefully, with the proceeds from the trail ride, not ever.

Moisture glistened in her eyes. "I don't know what to say. Does this mean you plan to stay on longer?"

"I'd like to. If you'll have me."

Her smile gained force. "I'd love that." She hugged him, then stiffened and pulled away. Blushing, she glanced about. "Honestly, I don't think we could survive without you."

"That's mighty good to know."

They stood, awkwardly staring at one another for a moment, before Rheanna politely excused herself to return to her "tour" with a promise to talk more later.

Unable to contain his grin, Dave emptied his wheelbarrow onto the compost pile, then headed to the tack room, which had become something of a store-all. Saddlebags and blankets and tangled ropes of various sizes lay on the ground. Others hung on hooks, along with various netting, bits and cribbing collars. Someone had decided to use an old grain bin as a garbage can.

He began sifting through a bunch of pop-up barrels and what looked like contractible laundry baskets, likely used in a jumping course, when bootsteps approached.

Rheanna?

Dusting his hands off, he walked out into the aisle.

He frowned. Sally Jo came toward him with that overly sugared smile he'd become much too familiar with. Her much-too-strong floral perfume preceded her.

He shoved a hand in his pocket. "Hey."

"Hi. I was hoping I'd run into you tonight."

Was that the sole reason she'd volunteered for the event? Surely, she wasn't that conniving.

He glanced past her. "Where's everyone else?"

"Asking a bunch of questions Rheanna's already answered."

And she thought that meant she needed to meander about the ranch on her own? "I best get back to my chores." He walked past her.

Her footsteps followed. "Dave, why are you acting this way?" Her voice carried a pout.

"Just getting stuff done, Sally Jo." He stepped out into the evening air and scanned the area for a sign of the other ladies. Bill was mending a section of barbed wire across the way, and Amelia was playing tug-of-war with T-Bone. "You might want to catch up with your crew."

"I already know what my job is."

"Which is?"

"Helping with the food. I'll be at the diner most of the time. Although I hope to pop over here to say hi, when I get the chance." She fingered a locket dangling from her gold necklace. "What do you have planned for tomorrow afternoon?"

"Why?"

"Boerne is hosting a German Street Fair today. Music, arts and crafts, food vendors. I thought it'd be fun if we—"

"I want to say this in a way that's both kind and clear. You and me? It's not going to happen. I'm not interested."

Her expression tightened. "Why? Because of Rheanna Stone? Do you really think she could ever love you if she knew what a lying coward you are? What would she say if I told her what you and your buddies did that night? That you were to blame for the death of that precious horse of hers?"

"That wasn't my fault."

"Really? Well, you certainly didn't do anything to prevent it. Not to mention I was the one. Me." She stabbed a thumb to her chest. "That you came running to after."

"It wasn't like that." Why had he talked to her that day at the gas station, that afternoon he and his family were heading out? Because the weight of it all had been squeezing him. Because she'd been there, acting all compassionate and kind, and he'd been a stupid, shell-shocked kid who felt like his world was tipping upside down.

"And then you left, running from Sage Creek so fast you thought that night would never catch up to you. Is that what you think? That you can just come back here and weasel into Rheanna's life like nothing happened. Like you and your no-good, partying friends weren't to blame for her grief? Did you really think she'd go for that?"

Dave stalked toward one of the ranch four-wheelers around back. "Leave me alone."

Once again, Sally Jo followed. "Oh, I'll leave you alone, all right. Pretty sure that naive girlfriend of yours will, too, once she learns about your dark little secret."

"What does that mean?" But he didn't have to ask. He could tell by her malicious tone she was planning on telling Rheanna everything.

He needed to talk to Rheanna. She needed to hear it from him, something that should've occurred long before now.

Unfortunately, Sally Jo got to her first, intersecting her as she and the others were heading to the ranch. He could tell by the way Sally Jo pulled Rheanna aside his secret was out, and likely an exaggerated version.

Dave jogged toward them. "Rheanna."

She stopped and stared at him. "Now's not the time, Dave."

His throat felt scratchy. He couldn't lose Rheanna over this. *Please, Lord, help me explain. Help her understand. Help her forgive me.*

When Rheanna ushered everyone inside for desserts, Dave sat in a rocker and waited for them to leave. He sat for thirty minutes, maybe more, mentally rehearsing what he would say. But what could he say? Rheanna had lost her horse, her best friend, because of him.

The door opened, and laughing women began spilling out, getting into their vehicles and driving away.

Sally Jo paused on the porch steps to give Dave a vindictive smile and wiggly finger wave. "Bye, y'all."

His muscles clenched. What had gotten into him, to ever date that woman? If he hadn't been such an angry, messed-up kid, he never would've.

Standing on the porch, Rheanna faced him. "Is it true? What she said?"

Dave's teeth ground together. Was Sally Jo so spiteful, she'd intentionally hurt someone else just to get back at him? But he knew she was. He'd seen that side of her on more than one occasion, back when they were kids. It was one of the biggest reasons he'd stopped dating her. He'd expected her to act hateful, once they broke up, but thankfully she'd started seeing someone else almost immediately and her obsession with Dave dramatically decreased.

"Did you kill Bella?"

"It's not like you think." The pain in her eyes sliced at his heart.

"Tell me what happened."

He had to be honest, and maybe if he and his family hadn't moved so quickly, he would've been, back when it had happened. At least, that's what he'd always told himself— that he would've told her but never got the chance. The truth was, he'd been afraid. Of getting into trouble, yes, but more than that, of disappointing the girl he loved.

The woman he loved.

"When your uncle kicked me and—" Phrasing it that way wouldn't help matters. "When he told my parents we needed to leave, I was mad. It didn't seem right or fair." It had also triggered past trauma from when his bio mom had been in crisis and the state had taken him from her.

He took in a deep, slow breath. "That night some

friends came over, a couple of kids I had no business hanging around. They brought liquor, and we holed up in the barn drinking and acting stupid. At some point, my buddies decided to take one of your uncle's tractors for a joyride. The keys were in it."

He closed his eyes and pinched the bridge of his nose. He should've known better—not to hang around those kids, not to take that first drink and certainly not to drink so much he lost all sense. "I should've stopped them, but I was too sloshed. At some point, I must've blacked out. I woke up the next morning facedown in a pile of hay."

"They killed Bella? They were the ones who ran her down?"

He took in a deep breath and nodded. "It was an accident."

"But you knew?"

"At first, I wasn't sure. But later, yeah. My buddy told me." Only because he was afraid he'd get in trouble and threatened to beat Dave up and blame it all on him if he told anyone.

Tears welled in her eyes. "You never told me. You wouldn't be telling now if not for Sally Jo. You knew how important Bella was to me."

He did, in a way only a few people, those who'd known how it felt to be completely alone, would. But that was precisely how Rheanna had felt that summer. Her mom had sent her off with little more than a cheery goodbye, to live with an uncle she felt certain didn't want her around. All the girls in Sage Creek had been jealous of her, making it hard for her to find friends. She'd told him all this in tears one day, after learning most of her Sunday school class had been invited to a party she'd been excluded from.

Then, drying her eyes, she'd wrapped her arms around

her horse's neck and said, *But I've got Bella.* Looking him in the eye, she added, *And you.*

He couldn't lose her. Not now, and not over something that had occurred nearly twenty years ago. "It was a terrible mistake, Rhe. You have to know that. I would never do anything to hurt you."

"But you never told me. Why? You were my friend. I trusted you."

"I'm sorry. Please, forgive me."

"I need time to process this."

Chapter Fourteen

The next morning, Rheanna woke up early to meet Sally Jo's grandmother, Mrs. Linn, at the diner to ensure they were set with food preparations. This was the big day, when all their planning would be put to the test. She couldn't believe how quickly they'd organized this event, and she knew she couldn't have done it without the help of the women at church.

Thankfully, Sally Jo hadn't arrived yet. Rheanna wasn't sure how she'd react around her. The woman had actually seemed to relish telling Rheanna about Dave's involvement in Bella's death. As if she'd received pleasure in inflicting pain.

Rheanna still hadn't made sense of his actions on that terrible night. Along with Bella, he'd been her best friend. He'd told her he loved her and had made so many promises—to always be there for her and to protect her. But he hadn't. He hadn't protected her from the loss of her beloved horse nor had he been honest about what had happened after her death.

"Rheanna, dear, sorry to keep you waiting."

She startled at the sound of Mrs. Linn's voice and stood to greet the diner's owner. "Ma'am." She shook her free hand, the other holding a tablet and pen. "Thank you so much for all you're doing to help with the trail ride."

"Of course. After everything those poor creatures suffered, how could I not? Besides, the local ranchers would done tan my hide, likely boycott this place, if I didn't." Dishes clanked in the kitchen behind her. "They told me they promised town folk would help out, if you took those horses on."

"They did." And they'd been right. Rheanna was amazed by all the support the community had shown her.

"Seems they're doing all they can to make good on that promise, even if that means strong-arming a few little old ladies." She winked. "But we're willing participants. Folks don't call this place horse country for nothing."

"I appreciate it. Is there anything you need from me?"

"Nope. Like I told you before, you can pay us on the back end. We're feeding about seventy-five, with maybe half those folks camping on the Owenses' property, correct?"

She nodded. They'd offered three levels of registration, each with differing costs: morning, full day or overnight. "And Mr. Hayes says everyone can picnic on a section of his land. He's got about an acre of pasture he's not currently using."

Mrs. Linn raised her eyebrows. "Really? Well, I'll be." She chuckled.

"You're sure this isn't too much?" And if she said yes? Then Rheanna would be in big trouble. Wilma's Diner would be providing lunch for everyone, volunteers included, and dinner for nearly fifty people. Rheanna had purchased packaged treats for morning and evening snacks to help lighten her load, but still.

Mrs. Linn smiled. "Not at all. I've got pert near the entire youth group slicing and dicing now. Plus, we're shutting this place down for the day. That way my staff and I can focus on the event. As for our workload—lunch won't be more than slapping bread, meat and cheese together. For supper, all we need to do is pour corn bread batter into pans and chili ingredients in pots."

"You are such a blessing and encouragement to me." She couldn't express how much.

Mrs. Linn's face softened, and she placed a hand over Rheanna's. "Today will be amazing. I have no doubt."

Rheanna smiled. She was starting to believe that.

And if Dave left? Could she still say that, especially considering she didn't have an instructor to take his place?

Mrs. Linn checked her watch. "I suppose I better get after it." She grinned, grabbed her things and stood.

Rheanna smiled. "Yeah, me, too." She reached out to offer a handshake, but Mrs. Linn pulled her into a hug instead.

"No formalities here, sweet girl." She softly patted Rheanna's cheek. "Now you best get back to that ranch of yours. Don't want folks showing up and you not there."

She laughed. "Good point."

While she anticipated some hiccups before the event ended, so far, everything seemed to be falling into place.

She mentally reviewed each component on her drive back to the ranch. Trinity Faith's quilting club had completely taken over everything related to registration and check-in. Faith and her "promotion" team had saturated the web and perhaps every bulletin board across the hill country with cleverly worded advertisements. Drake and his buddies had ensured all the trails were connected and clearly marked. His folks and a few of their friends were preparing their property for campers and a cookout. Pastor Roger had even finagled an a capella group to provide evening entertainment.

By the time she arrived at the house, numerous volunteers were waiting for her.

Showtime.

She took in a deep breath to calm her jittery nerves and stepped out of her vehicle. Two of the girls from youth group ran toward her, immediately bombarding her with questions.

"Good morning, ladies." She glanced around for Lucy. The older woman stood in front of the porch steps, clipboard in hand, addressing a group of women from Sage Creek's cultural committee. Catching the woman's eye, Rheanna smiled and waved, then shifted toward the teens. "I need to pop into the stables really quickly. But Mrs. Carr will be able to answer all your questions."

That woman had been such a godsend from the moment she and her "welcome wagon" as they liked to call themselves had stopped by the ranch. But for this event especially. The woman was so competent, Rheanna had no doubt, if, for any reason, she had to step away, Lucy could run the trail ride without her.

With a prayer of thanks, Rheanna grabbed a water bottle from a tub en route and marched off toward where they kept their boarders. She found Bill loading fresh hay into a wheelbarrow.

Upon seeing her, he staked his pitchfork in the ground and rested an arm on its handle. "Ma'am."

His frown suggested he wasn't any more pleased with their trail ride event this morning than he had been when she first told him about it. Then again, he never had been the cheerful type.

"Thought I'd stop in and see if you needed anything before the chaos starts." She gave a nervous laugh.

He shook his head. "Been working with horses since before you were born, Ms. Stone."

Her face heated at what felt like a jab at her inexperience. But his comment could only prick her insecurities if she let it, and she had no intention of doing that. "I'm very appreciative of all your experience, today especially, with Dave and I being tied up with the event and all."

"Along with the Dillard boys."

"Right." That meant Bill would have to clean all the stalls himself, although she suspected Dave had woken extra early to take care of those belonging to the rescues. That was kind of his way. And while she appreciated that about him, his betrayal still stung. He may not have outright lied to her, but withholding the information felt the same.

He set his pitchfork on top of his mound of hay. "Just hope all this rope-de-dope is worth it."

She couldn't help but think that was his way of stating that he found all her efforts a waste of time, if not a drain on ranch man-hours.

What if he was right? They'd received a good number of registrations, hopefully some of which would lead to long-term business. They'd also managed to rent space to a fair number of vendors and would receive a percentage on their sales along with some kickbacks from Drake's camping rentals and food purchases.

It still wasn't sufficient to cover all her expenses but it was a start, and maybe just enough of one to save the ranch.

"I have faith this will all work out precisely as God intends." She hoped her smile conveyed much more confidence than she felt.

Bill mumbled something and walked away, pushing his wheelbarrow, making it clear precisely what he thought of her and her ranch-saving efforts.

With a sigh, she strode out of the stables, giving her-

self the same pep talk she planned to give her volunteers
momentarily.

Turning toward the house, she nearly smacked into
Dave. "Oh." She startled and stepped back, then stiffened. "Excuse me."

"Can we talk?"

She studied him for a minute, wanting to say yes, to
fix the rift between them, and wanting just as strongly
to leave. Because if she closed her heart to romance for
good, then she wouldn't get hurt.

But this was Dave, and regardless of where they went
from here, she needed to hear him out.

She nodded.

He gazed past her for a long moment, as if struggling
with what to say, or maybe how to begin. Then he released
a breath and met her eye. "I know I messed up. Big-time.
I messed up when I invited those troublemakers over.
I messed up when I took that first swig and even more
when I watched my buddies drain the bottle. I'd like to
sit here and say I didn't know what would happen, but I
can't. Maybe I didn't know about Bella, but I knew how
they got when drunk. Only I didn't care. I was too caught
up in my own hurt and anger.

"Telling you how much I regret that night or that I
haven't taken a drop of booze since I became a follower
of Jesus won't undo what's been done." He rubbed his
thumb knuckle with his other thumb. "And you're right,
I should've told you. I wanted to. Once I found out. But
I was scared."

She huffed. "Of what? Getting in trouble and having
to pay a fine?"

"Of losing you."

She crossed her arms. "If that were true, you wouldn't
have left so easily."

"I didn't have a choice. Your uncle—"

"Because of Bella? Did he find out what happened?"

"I don't think so. He may have suspected, but if he did, he never said anything. Least, not that I know of."

He could have talked with Dave's parents. He and Dave's dad could've gotten into an argument. That made sense, with how suddenly his family had left. "You said we'd stay together. That no one and nothing, not even hundreds of miles, could tear us apart." Her voice cracked. "That you'd fight for me, write to me and call me."

"I did. I must've sent at least a dozen letters. Didn't you get them?"

She shook her head, combing her memory back to that time. Everything had unraveled so quickly. Him leaving, her cancer diagnosis and treatment. That was when she'd needed to hear from Dave most.

Had he truly written, and if so, why hadn't she known?

Boys like that ain't nothing but trouble. Her uncle's statement, made the day the two of them stood on his sagging porch, watching Dave and his family drive away, resurfaced. She knew her uncle had disliked Dave, but enough to intercept her mail? And if all that hadn't happened—Dave's moving, her uncle's subterfuge, her cancer and hospitalization—would Dave have told her about Bella?

"Why did my uncle make you and your parents leave?"

A flash of pain lit his eyes, and for a moment, his gaze wavered, as if he knew the answer to her question but didn't want to share it. Why?

"Dave, please. No more secrets."

"Your uncle sold the land my dad had been renting. To pay for your cancer treatment." He looked in the distance, as if controlling his emotions before speaking, then focused on her once again. "I didn't know, Rhe, that you were sick. I wish I had. I wish I'd known why your uncle sent us packing, too. It makes sense now. He was helping you."

She sucked in a breath and jerked back. How could that be? Her uncle hadn't even liked her all that much.

Except... He'd taken her in. Fed her dinner each night, lectured her regarding boys and men every chance that he got.

And kept Dave from her, the person she loved more than anything.

Rheanna had always figured her uncle saw the worst in her and assumed she was just like her mother. But what if what she saw as disdain was actually love? Then Rheanna hadn't been abandoned, not by him.

Maybe not by Dave, either.

"Whether you forgive me or not—" Dave's voice sounded husky "—I still plan to help. In any way I can, for as long as you'll let me."

"I forgive you. I just..." She shook her head, unable to verbalize all she was feeling. But her heart hurt. "What does that mean for us?"

"I know I don't have a right to ask." He swallowed. "But are you okay now? Your appointment in Houston—"

"I'm fine. That was just a follow-up to watch for secondary cancers."

"They're worried about that?"

She didn't want to concern him, but neither would she lie to him. "I have an increased risk, but not enough to fret about."

He studied her for a long moment, then gave one quick nod.

Silence stretched between them. She wanted to be angry at her uncle, and in a way, she was. But she also understood his behavior. How might she have acted, had she been in his place and Amelia in hers?

Did this change anything between her and Dave? He'd still played a huge part in the death of her horse, then had kept that from her. She knew precisely where relational secrets led—her ex-husband had kept plenty, and she'd been too blinded by "love" to notice the warning signs.

Was she doing that with Dave, as well? If not now, would she? Her heart said she could trust him, and she wanted to, but her head wasn't sure. For Amelia's sake, Rheanna needed to be certain.

Someone called her name, and she turned to see all her volunteers gathered and waiting for her. "I've got to go."

With a heavy heart, Dave watched Rheanna jog toward the house.

Just when he had begun to believe Rheanna was beginning to trust him, to love him, again... Had he blown things between them for good? What if she told him to leave?

That would be twice he'd been kicked off this place, only this time he'd only have himself to blame.

With a sigh, he shuffled toward the stables to ready their "rental" horses. He'd just led the last of the mares out to pasture when his phone rang.

He glanced at the screen. It was Rheanna. "Hello?"

"The vet called. Asha had her foal."

He exhaled a laugh, then he sobered. Surely her wound hadn't had time to heal yet. "What about her incision?"

"He was worried about that, too, which is why she delivered via C-section."

Should they have gone that route from the beginning? They'd considered it but had opted to give the baby as much time in Asha's womb as possible. "How's she doing? Did they both make it out of surgery?"

"So far so good. Mom's resting and baby's already fighting to stand."

"Should we drive over there?"

"He suggested we not, in part because of the trail ride, I'm sure. But he assured me he had the situation handled and would call us if there was any change."

"How soon does he think mom and baby will come home?"

"Most likely within the next three to five days."

"Okay." She didn't say more, but neither did she end the call.

Was she thinking of their conversation from earlier?

"Rheanna...?"

"I've got to go."

This time, she hung up.

Lord, I know I messed up, and I probably have no right to ask, but if You'd fix the mess I made of things, I'd be awful grateful. Don't let me lose that sweet woman You so graciously brought back into my life. Or her daughter.

Moping around wouldn't do him any good. Right now, the best way he could help both Stone ladies was to tackle the last of his chores so he could help with the event. He'd just finished giving a mash mixture to the last of the rescues when the patter of feet slapped on the concrete behind him.

"Eat up, little lady." He scratched the mare's withers, pleased when she didn't pull away. Then he exited the stall.

Amelia stood in the aisle, barefoot and in her pajamas, panting, cheeks flushed. Her hair spilled out of her ponytail, with stray, mussed locks framing her face. She clutched papers and tape in her arms. "Mister Dave, did you hear? Asha had her baby!"

He laughed. "I heard, muffin-girl." He swept her hair from her eyes. "Good news, huh?"

Her head bobbed. "Mama said she can't come home just yet, but that's okay. 'Cause that gives us more time, right?"

"For?"

"To decorate her stall! That's what people do when babies are born, silly." She proceeded to tell him about all the pictures she'd made. "I don't have money for balloons, so I made some." She held up a brightly colored page. "Do you think she'll mind? And Mama said horses can't have cake, not even peppermint-flavored ones."

He fought to keep from chuckling. "True, and I don't think Asha's little one will mind about the balloons at all."

"Can I still help with her? The baby, I mean? Getting her used to people touching her with their hands and stuff?"

"Handling?"

She nodded.

"I sure hope so." He winked, smiling at the pure pleasure that lit her eyes. That was one of the things he loved most about Amelia. She was sure easy to please. Just give her something useful to do, let her know you believed she could do it and she acted like a guy promised her a dollhouse. Or cakeless frosting.

Another set of footfalls approached, and he glanced up to find Rheanna marching toward them. "Amelia, what are you doing out here?" Her words were breathless, and her gaze pinged to his. "One minute she was bugging me to help her find her new cowgirl boots, the next she was gone. I suppose I should've figured she'd be out here with you." Sorrow weighted her tone.

She was wounded, largely because of him, when he'd been trying so hard *not* to hurt her.

She'd experienced so much pain and rejection, well before they'd ever met. That was what had originally drawn them together. Trust was hard-won and easily broken for the both of them.

Had he shattered hers beyond repair? Proven whatever nagging suspicions she had regarding him, and men in general, true?

He refused to believe that. Refused to let her go. If only he could convince her of that, then maybe she'd have the courage to heal.

"My property will be listed by the end of the day."

She studied him with a furrowed brow. "What does that mean?"

"God willing, we should have the money to pay off the ranch's IRS debts by month's end, if not sooner."

"We should talk about that."

Did she think he'd change his mind, if she decided they were through? That his help was conditional? "As far as I'm conc—"

"Mister Dave!" Amelia tugged on his arm, leaning all her fifty pounds toward Asha's empty stall. "Help me tape these up. Please."

"Sure."

"Yay!" She released his arm and raced down the aisle, dropping one of her pictures as she went. It fluttered to the ground.

Rheanna took a visible breath. "I need to get back to the house anyway."

He nodded and fell into step beside her, pausing when she stopped to pick up Amelia's fallen paper. On it, she'd drawn three stick figures holding hands, child in the center, all three flanked by a horse on each side.

His heart gave a painful squeeze as he remembered his conversation with Rheanna on the day they'd kissed. This was precisely why she hadn't wanted to become romantically involved with him. But he didn't plan on hurting that precious girl, not her or her mother. Nor did he plan on leaving the ranch.

Chapter Fifteen

Rheanna spent the rest of the morning directing their guests where to go while trying to keep an eye on Amelia. Thankfully, her volunteers had everything else managed. She had a team staffing check-in, others directing traffic and still others pairing those who arrived without horses with mounts.

Ten of these belonged to Rheanna, and per Lucy's suggestion, half wore a lightweight banner advertising her ranch and riding lessons. The other half advertised her rescue efforts, not that she found this necessary, considering everyone knew the reason for this event. Thanks to Sage Creek's youth, today's trail ride had nearly gone viral.

Hugging a clipboard to her chest, Lucy approached in jean shorts and an orange tank top.

Rheanna handed a volunteer a box of single-serving bagged chips, then faced her friend. "Is there a problem?" Lucy's concerned expression worried her.

She gave a quick nod. "The ponies you rented are going to be late."

Rheanna checked the time on her phone. "What do you mean?"

"Apparently their trailer got a flat, and they think it'll take them forty-five minutes or so to fix it."

"That long to put on a spare?"

"I got the feeling the guys driving are fairly young and inexperienced, a couple hired hands more than likely."

Rheanna rubbed her collarbone. "We've got other horses, but I'm not sure I trust them for an event like this. Bill's still training about half of them, and the others... I just feel better using our lesson horses."

"I agree, considering we're using this event for advertising, as well."

"But I also don't want to keep people waiting that long."

Lucy angled her head and tapped her chin. "How about you create a little pre-show entertainment?"

"What do you mean?"

"Where's Dave?" She glanced around, then brightened. "There he is. Hold up." She trotted off.

"Girl, what are you up to?"

Lucy tossed a grin over her shoulder. "Don't worry. I've got this."

Less than fifteen minutes later, volunteers were directing horses and riders into one of their grazing pastures for a "free group lesson." Rheanna followed and watched as Dave turned what she'd originally viewed as a disaster into a booking opportunity. He demonstrated how to canter, talked about ways to calm a nervous horse, engage a "lazy" horse and how to counter certain behavioral problems.

By the time he finished, the ponies had arrived and numerous trail riders had asked about lessons.

Rheanna took Lucy's megaphone. "As a way to show our appreciation to you all for coming out and supporting our cause, we're running a trail riders' special. Book

two lessons today and receive your third one free." By
then, Dave would have them hooked and eager for more.

She'd miss him, if he left. But could she handle it if he
stayed? Not if he did so as a friend or employee. Her heart
had moved past that, and she couldn't pretend it hadn't.
But could she trust him to be more?

"Mama." Amelia ran toward her wearing the adorable
cowgirl hat—pink with a large glittered star and bejeweled
band encircling the crown. "Can I go with Mister Dave?"

T-Bone followed her, stopped near her feet, then scurried off toward a table Lucy had lined with doughnuts
and refreshments.

Rheanna's chest stung at the reminder of how close
her daughter and Dave had become. She glanced toward
where Dave stood, talking with lingering riders who'd
participated in his class. "He's going to be busy with the
trail riders, sweetie." They'd already talked about him
leading the endeavor with Rheanna and some others picking up the rear.

"Not too busy for me." She crossed her arms with such
an exaggerated frown, Rheanna could hardly keep from
laughing.

"Oh, is that right? What makes you so sure?"

"Because that's what he always tells me. That he's never
too busy for 'his little buddy.'"

Oh, sweet Amelia. If only she didn't attach so quickly
and easily. "I'll talk to him."

Amelia skipped and galloped alongside her as she made
her way toward Dave. She reached him just as he was exiting and latching the now-empty pasture area.

Upon seeing her, he halted, and a shadow of pain tinged
with hope filled his eyes. But then, shifting his attention
to Amelia, he donned his familiar boyish grin.

"Look at you, Ms. Cowgirl." He squeezed the crown of her hat.

"You like my new hat?"

"Love it. You'll be the prettiest gal on the trails, that's for sure."

Amelia straightened with a smile so wide, her face practically glowed. "Can I ride with you?"

His gaze shot to Rheanna and lingered, causing her pulse to accelerate, which only added to her conflicting emotions. She wanted to trust him, but she'd loved and lost too much in her lifetime. As had her daughter.

Dave scratched his chin. "What's your mama say?"

"That you're too busy." Amelia's tone let them both know precisely how silly she found that notion. "But you're not, are you? You're never too busy for me."

He smiled and gave her a side squeeze. "How about your mama and I talk for a minute."

Amelia let out such a dramatic sigh, her entire torso flopped forward. "All right."

He and Rheanna moved out of earshot.

"I don't mind taking her." He rested a hand on his shiny belt buckle. "Having her near wouldn't cause any problems, and she's a good enough rider to manage her own."

He looked like he wanted to say more, but instead, he simply waited, deep soft eyes latched on hers.

She nodded. "Okay."

Amelia was thrilled, and soon Dave had her mounted on one of their older and more patient and obedient horses and gathered with the others near their trailhead. While he gave last minute information to everyone, including when and where they'd be stopping for lunch, Rheanna checked with Lucy to ensure everything else was set.

Lucy grinned. "Everything's going as smooth as my grandma's custard pie on the Fourth of July. In fact, all you've got to do is get on that horse of yours and enjoy the day."

She gave her friend a hug. "I don't know what I'd do without you. Seriously."

"And what about me without you? I'd be sitting home, bored, forced to spend my time eating chocolate and watching sappy old reruns. Which I still might do, once this is all over." She winked and waltzed off to the registration table, where their teen volunteers were gathering their things.

Convinced she wasn't needed, Rheanna mounted her horse and followed the last of the trail riders entering the treed area of her property. The rest of the day went more smoothly than she could've dreamed. At their lunch spot, some of Trinity Faith's youth had set up a "photo op" area and were ready with a camera and sign that read #rheannashorserescue. Upon Rheanna's consent, they were using social media to host a giveaway—a sizable basket of donated goodies. To enter, riders simply needed to post fun pictures of themselves enjoying the event using their designated hashtag.

Rheanna waited for a family of four to finish taking photos, then approached the girls. "You ladies are brilliant. What a way to generate free advertising."

Tiana Marshal, a sophomore with long red hair pulled into a ponytail, blew a bubble, then let it pop. "We're going to make you go viral. Just you wait."

"Oh, I know a way to make this event go viral." Hunter grinned.

"Based on all those goofy videos I've seen already, I can only imagine," Rheanna said, as she climbed back onto her horse.

Then, leaving the teens to continue their plotting and planning, she returned to the trail, this time heading past the Cedar View Inn to Mr. Farmer's place. From there, they'd continue on to the Owenses' ranch, where some of them would be tent camping while a handful of others were sleeping in the historical bed-and-breakfast. Thankfully, Rheanna would be part of the latter. She'd never been able to sleep outside, or on the hard ground for that matter.

But she was looking forward to tonight's cookout and bonfire. The music, the s'mores, sharing stories and jokes…

Seeing Dave, the person she'd last sat around a bonfire with. They'd gone with other kids from school. She couldn't remember who'd officially been invited, nor did it matter. Neither her nor Dave had felt all that connected with the local teens. Plus, Rheanna had still been in her shy, awkward phase, intensified by the rejection and abandonment she'd carried into town.

But with Dave she had felt different. Safe. Accepted. Beautiful.

Loved.

Honestly, he still had a way of making her feel beautiful, and maybe even loved. But safe enough to give him her heart?

After a long, hot day of trail riding, Dave told his group to check out the vendors, then used that time to rehydrate himself and the horses. Once done, he headed to the bonfire area to help with setup.

By the time the sun dipped below the tree line, sparks of yellow and orange crackled while smoke billowed toward the starlit sky. The scent of roasting marshmallows, laughter and conversation merged with the normal night sounds and smells of the hill country.

He glanced about for Rheanna and found her sitting

next to one of her friends from church. She held Amelia on her lap, and based on the way the child snuggled in close, she was clearly tired. Then again, he'd noticed her wilting about an hour before supper. Seeing her droopy-eyed expression and flushed cheeks from the long day's ride had triggered something paternal within him. Made him even more determined not to lose what the good Lord had been building here.

This had to be from God, for him and Rheanna to reconnect as they had. And maybe even her finding out about Bella was, too, so that there'd be no secrets between them. And God willing, no guilt.

When Rheanna's friend got up, Dave ambled over. "Mind if I sit?"

At first, she looked like she was going to turn him away, but then she gave a slight nod. "Thank you for all you did today. With Amelia, leading the trail ride, the group lessons this morning."

"We're booked for lessons for the next month."

"Seriously?"

"Yep. And I suspect by the time this little shindig is over, we'll have quite a waiting list." Surely that meant she wouldn't ask him to leave, especially considering she still didn't have a replacement. Except one of the riders, a guy from one town over, had been asking about employment opportunities, saying he'd worked with horses all his life.

Dave had lingered, hoping to catch Rheanna's response, until a lady started asking him questions regarding how to handle an aggressive horse. He shouldn't have been frustrated by the interruption, considering he likely received a new student. But the uncertainty between him and Rheanna, the possibility of losing her, was eating at him.

Elbows on his knees, he leaned toward her. "Listen, Rheanna—"

"Hey, everyone." The tallest of the homeschooled trip-lets stood in the center of the campfire circle, clanking a stick against a soda can. "As most of you know, I'm Hunter and my brothers and I have been working on Ms. Rheanna's ranch for going on five months now. At first, we weren't too keen on the place, or Ms. Rheanna." He shifted his focus her way. "No offense, ma'am. But that was before we got to know her or see what she was about. What she's capable of."

Dave cast Rheanna a sideways glance. She'd dropped her gaze as she often did when folks tried to praise her, and her cheeks blushed pink in the faint glow of the fire.

"When we first saw those rescues…" The kid whistled. "Honestly, we didn't think they stood a chance. I was sur-prised they made it past that first week. But they did. And even now, they just keep getting stronger."

"Thanks to our resident horse whisperer," someone to Dave's left called out, eliciting claps and exclamations of agreement.

"Anyway," the teen continued, "my brothers and I are right proud to be working on the ranch and hope we can for years to come. As you can see, it's for purely selfish reasons that we created a Fund-Me-Easy campaign, and with the help of our social media obsessed friends…" He shot a pointed look tinged with mirth to a group of girls sitting kitty-corner to him. "I'm happy to say we've been able to raise thirty thousand dollars."

"What?" Rheanna's word came out on a gasp, and Dave blinked.

Thirty thousand dollars? Raised by a pack of meme-and video-sharing teens? Wow. These Sage Creek folks were something else. Looking at Rheanna, he squeezed her hand, though what he really wanted to do was scoop her up and hold her close.

She swiped her fingers beneath her teary eyes and offered a watery smile.

Lucy came near and draped an arm over Rheanna's shoulder. "And that's not all, my hardworking, stubborn, tenacious friend. Wait until you see how much we pulled in this weekend, with folks paying extra right and left. Seems all our prayers paid off, huh? And like I told you when you first came and were thinking maybe you weren't cut out for ranching life—God didn't bring you here to leave you stranded."

"I don't know what to say."

"Thank You will suffice," Lucy said.

"Thank you."

"Oh, no. Not to me." She pointed to the sky, then straightened. "That little one of yours is plumb worn-out. How about I get her tucked in for the night? She's sleeping with you at the Owenses' place, right?"

Rheanna nodded. "Again, thank you." She nudged Amelia awake. "Hey, sweetie. You ready for bed?"

Amelia groaned, rubbed an eye with her fist and nodded.

Rheanna kissed her cheek. "Go with Ms. Lucy."

Once her daughter and Lucy left, Rheanna shook her head. "I'm struggling to believe all this," she told Dave. "I mean, I know, when you and those ranchers first brought the horses, those men said everyone would help. But—"

"But you figured they were just making promises they had no intention of keeping."

"Oh, I knew they meant it in the moment, but sometimes good intentions aren't enough."

He understood what she was saying, and also got the sense that she was talking about more than horses and Sage Creek residents.

"And your ranch. I was deeply touched that you were

willing to sell it. It showed me how very much you love those horses. I know you'd do anything for them."

"I wasn't selling for them. Well, I was. But more than that, I was doing it for you. And not just because I owe you. I wish I could go back to that night when Bella died. I wish I'd never gotten drunk, that I'd never invited those friends over. And I wish my family and I had never left Sage Creek, but we did." He brushed his knuckles against her soft cheek. "I wish I would've told you. You deserved that."

"I'm not mad at you, Dave. I'm just..." Tears once again glimmered in her eyes. "This isn't just about me. Amelia's already had one man walk out on her."

As had Rheanna—more than once. "I'm not going anywhere. Not unless you tell me to, and even then, I'll fight you on it. Because I love you. I always have, but spending time with you again... I love you more than ever, and I know without a doubt that I want to spend the rest of my life with you. And Amelia. If you'll let me."

"I want to trust you. I really do, and that scares me. Because if I let you in, it has to be for forever."

He patted his back pocket, searching for the ring he'd placed there, but then he remembered he'd tucked it into his backpack so it wouldn't fall out on the trail.

"Hold on." He chided himself for breaking what otherwise might've been a romantic moment and dashed to where he'd deposited his gear at the base of a tree.

He returned to Rheanna out of breath, from his haste and nerves. If she said no? He'd be crushed. There'd been a time when he would've done anything to avoid the sting of rejection, of opening his heart to someone only to lose them. But for Rheanna, he was willing to risk the pain.

"Rheanna." His throat felt scratchy. He cleared it,

clammy hand closed around the soft velvet box he'd kept among other long-cherished items.

That box had been the first thing he'd pulled from the flood, and he'd kept it with him since. In it, he had a photo of him and his mom, taken when he was three or four, before the state took him away. And among a handful of other cherished mementos and notes, he'd saved a simple yet elegant ring.

It'd been a gift from his biological grandmother, given to him the first and last time she'd seen him. *This is a promise of love, and you must hold tight to it*, she'd said. *Hold tight to this promise, but even more, to love once you find it. And you will find it.*

"Rheanna," he said again, and lowered to one knee, "I want this to be forever, to hold tight to you for forever, if you'll let me."

"What are you saying?"

"Rheanna Stone." He revealed a vintage rose gold ring with a halo diamond, then grabbed her slender hand. "Will you marry me?"

Her eyes widened, and she covered her mouth with her free hand. His heart thudded as he waited for her answer, and he suddenly became alert to the silence, other than the cackling fire, all around him.

She gave a whimpered laugh and nodded.

"Is that a yes?"

"Dave Brewster, it's a yes."

Folks cheered, and he sprang to his feet. "Woo-hoo!" He scooped Rheanna up so that her back rested against one arm and her legs dangled over the other.

Chapter Sixteen

One year later

Rheanna stood in front of the cheval mirror Lucy had brought from her bedroom and ran a hand down the bodice of her gown. It was off-white with spaghetti straps, open-backed, and had a thick band of intricately threaded beads at her waist. The bottom hem hit her midcalf in front with a two-foot-long train.

Casting a glance Lucy's way, she stepped into her pink ballerina flats, which were also embellished with beads. "This dress might not have been the best choice for a horse-ride wedding."

"Pshaw." Lucy grabbed the floral bouquet lying on the coffee table and straightened its encircling ribbon. "You're beautiful. That cowboy of yours won't hardly know what to do with himself. You just might render him speechless. Besides, you'll be riding sidesaddle."

"Where's Amelia?" She crossed to the window and parted the curtains ever-so-slightly. "She promised she'd only be gone a moment."

"Most likely she's 'schooling' Little Lady on how this afternoon's going to go."

Rheanna laughed. "Or trying to teach her to walk on cue." Amelia had become rather obsessed with Asha's foal, ever since they brought the feisty creature home. In fact, Dave had encouraged the child to practically take over all handling, and she'd been doing a phenomenal job. She'd grown as attached to Little Lady as Rheanna had to the foal's mother—and her love for the horse equaled all she'd once felt for Bella.

Lucy checked her phone screen. "Maybe I should go hunt her down." She made a visual scan first of Rheanna, then of their surroundings. "Seems we're all set here."

Minus Ivy. Rheanna frowned. And if her former best friend didn't show? Though the wedding would go on, obviously, and the day would still be amazing, it'd be tinged with the sadness of a broken relationship unrestored.

With a sigh, Rheanna dabbed her nose and forehead with a tissue, then reapplied a soft dusting of facial powder.

"Let's pray." Doris, a member of Trinity Faith's quilting club, took Rheanna's hand in hers, then motioned for everyone else to form a circle. Once they had, she bowed her head, thanked God for all He'd done in the past year and asked for His blessings on every day thereafter.

Before she concluded, the front door flew open. "Mama, Aunt Ivy's here." Amelia burst in with bright eyes, staticky hair and rosy cheeks. Ivy followed close behind, wearing shorts and a T-shirt and carrying a garment bag in one hand and blush-toned sandals in the other.

Upon seeing Rheanna, her eyes instantly filled with tears. "Oh, wow. Girl, look at you." She greeted her with a tight hug void of any lingering hostility or hurt.

Rheanna blew a burst of air upward to keep from crying herself. She had no intention of causing her mascara to run. "Thanks for coming."

"Well, you know, free food and all." She gave her signature mischievous smile, then, with a look to Amelia, raised her garment bag. "Come on, lil one. Let's you and I put our princess gear on."

"Yeah!" She bounced on her feet, then skipped after Ivy toward the bedroom, chattering as she went. "Did you know Mama and Mister Dave are getting married on horses? And Little Lady, that's my horse, and I are the flower girls. I've been teaching her to lead."

A knock sounded on the door, and a moment later Hunter poked his head in. "Ma'am, Asha's ready."

Rheanna sucked in a deep breath and released it slowly. "Thank you."

She turned to Lucy. "I guess it's showtime, huh?" She glanced toward the hallway, wondering how long it'd take Ivy and Amelia to get ready.

"We'll tend to those two." Lucy motioned to herself and Doris. "Won't take but a minute. Dress on, hair tucked in that precious bonnet Mrs. Hayes adorned for her, and she'll be ready to go."

"Thank you." Rheanna gathered her train to keep from tripping on it and stepped outside into the warm summer air. The aroma of sun-roasted hay and earth wafted toward her, and a gentle breeze soothed her with the scent of lilac.

Her phone chimed a text, and she glanced at the screen and smiled. It was from Dave's dad, saying he was ready and "all fancied up in a real live tuxedo."

Some might consider Dave's dad "giving her away" too nontraditional, but she hadn't known how to handle her lack of a father figure. Besides, he'd been more of a dad to her than any other male she'd known. And by the end of the day, he'd technically be her dad anyway. She was so grateful Amelia would never have to deal with such issues.

Hunter stood in the center of the grass, holding Asha by

her halter. The mare looked freshly groomed, white satin ribbon had been braided into her tail, and her muscular frame showed no signs of her previous maltreatment. Placing a hand on Asha's withers, Rheanna was overcome with emotion as she thought of how far the horse had come.

How far they all had come, actually. And after today, their lives would be bound, inseparably together. *Thank You, Lord, for the gift of healing and second chances.*

Hunter helped her into her saddle, then led her to the side of the barn and out of view of Dave while they waited for the rest of the wedding party. His dad approached a few moments later wearing a periwinkle blue tuxedo, a cowboy hat and boots.

Rheanna smiled. "You clean up good."

Mr. Brewster gave her a side hug. "You don't look too shabby yourself. You nervous?"

"A little. Mostly that I'll fall off, but more than that, I'm excited."

"I used to wonder what might become of Dave and his book-reading girl from the city. I could tell he loved you from the start. And I kind of had an inclination that maybe you loved him back."

She had, and did.

Amelia's chattering voice reached them a moment before she did, leading her foal, the ring basket strapped to his saddle blanket, as she came. Ivy and Lucy followed close behind, both dressed in long, ruby-colored satin gowns.

The soft plink of the harp signaled the ceremony had begun. Amelia giggled, then patted Little Lady on the neck. "You ready, girl?"

Rheanna's heart felt ready to explode with joy as she watched her princess confidently lead the foal she'd been working so hard to train. Thanks to Dave.

Dear Reader,

I wrote this story, about a rancher who saw his ranch destroyed after massive flooding swept through his town, while those in my community were still recovering from equal devastation. Perhaps you saw the news of all that occurred in Nebraska and Iowa in the spring of 2019. If you did, I imagine you grieved with all of us. What the media failed to show, however, was how the community banded together in such amazing ways and the love, strength and perseverance displayed by so many of our ranchers and farmers. They are the inspiration for this story.

Like Rheanna, we all need others to help sometimes. And they need us to help them, too. Building such close, interdependent relationships may feel frightening initially, but they are well worth the risk. I'd love to connect with you on Facebook or Instagram—just search for my name. You can also find me at JenniferSlatteryLivesOutLoud.com.

Thanks for picking up my book!
Jennifer

COMING NEXT MONTH FROM
Love Inspired

SNOWBOUND WITH THE AMISH BACHELOR
Redemption's Amish Legacies • by Patricia Johns

When social worker Grace Schweitzer arrives at the Hochstetler family farm to pick up an abandoned baby, a blizzard leaves her stranded. Grace has no plans to return to the Amish life she left behind, but soon she's losing her heart to bachelor Ben Hochstetler *and* the faith she once held dear.

HIS AMISH WIFE'S HIDDEN PAST
by Mindy Steele

Englischer Hannah Raber will do anything to protect her children when they are sent into witness protection—even marry her late husband's brother. But learning to be an Amish wife to Daniel is an adjustment. Can these strangers from different worlds turn a convenient marriage into a forever love?

FINDING A CHRISTMAS HOME
Rescue Haven • by Lee Tobin McClain

As the new guardian to her twin nieces, Hannah Antonicelli is determined to keep her promise to her late sister—that she'll never reveal the identity of their father. But when the twins' uncle, Luke Hutchenson, is hired as a handyman at her job and begins to bond with the little girls, keeping the secret isn't easy...

HER HOLIDAY SECRET
Cowboys of Diamondback Ranch • by Jolene Navarro

As a pregnant teen, Catalina Wimberly sacrificed everything to protect Andres Sanchez's future. Now she's temporarily back in town to tell him he's a father. There's no doubt he'll love their five-year-old daughter, but will he ever be able to forgive Catalina?

A SAFE PLACE FOR CHRISTMAS
by Lisa Carter

When Christmas tree farmer Luke Morgan finds his childhood friend Shayla Coggins and her baby in their broken-down car during a snowstorm, he offers them a place to stay for the holidays. But while her son draws the pair together, Shayla's dark secret threatens to end their budding romance.

THE FAMILY HE NEEDS
by Lorraine Beatty

From the moment Joy Duncan goes to work for reclusive Simon Baker, their relationship is contentious—despite his instant bond with her little boy. But Joy begins to wonder if there's more to Simon beneath his pain and anger. Could this hurting widower be the father and husband her little family needs?

LOOK FOR THESE AND OTHER LOVE INSPIRED BOOKS WHEREVER BOOKS ARE SOLD, INCLUDING MOST BOOKSTORES, SUPERMARKETS, DISCOUNT STORES AND DRUGSTORES.

LICNM0921

Get 4 **FREE REWARDS!**

We'll send you 2 FREE Books
plus 2 FREE Mystery Gifts.

Love Inspired books feature uplifting stories where faith helps guide you through life's challenges and discover the promise of a new beginning.

FREE
Value Over
$20

IF YOU ENJOYED THIS BOOK, DON'T MISS NEW EXTENDED-LENGTH NOVELS FROM LOVE INSPIRED!

In addition to the Love Inspired books you know and love, we're excited to introduce even more uplifting stories in a longer format, with more inspiring fresh starts and page-turning thrills!

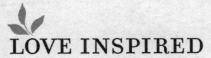

LOVE INSPIRED

Stories to uplift and inspire.

Fall in love with Love Inspired—inspirational and uplifting stories of faith and hope. Find strength and comfort in the bonds of friendship and community. Revel in the warmth of possibility, and the promise of new beginnings.

LOOK FOR THESE LOVE INSPIRED TITLES ONLINE AND IN THE BOOK DEPARTMENT OF YOUR FAVORITE RETAILER!